The Crow Foretells a Stormy Day

T. Edward Abbott

Tiny Boar Books   Port Townsend, WA   2021

Tiny Boar Books
Water Street
Port Townsend, WA 98368
www.tinyboarbooks.com

The Library of Congress has catalogued this edition as follows:
Abbott, T. Edward
The crow foretells a stormy day / T. Edward Abbott -1st Tiny Boar Books ed.
1. Magical Realism—Fiction. 2. Fairy Tales, Folk Tales, Legends & Mythology—Fiction. 3. Horror—Fiction.
Library of Congress Control Number: 2021906868

ISBN-13: 978-1-955290-00-5 (paperback)

Titles by T. Edward Abbott

On the Nature of Things

The Crow Foretells a Stormy Day

Exile, or, A Tale of Enchantment in Eight Parts

The Crow Foretells a Stormy Day

Contents

ICE

MARTIN lived on the top floor of an eighteenth-century walk-up in a neighborhood separated from the rest of the city by a viaduct expressway that never ceased howling. Though antiquated, the building was not picturesque. The ivy that had dislodged most of the bricks from the façade had languished on the edge of extinction for years. A cracked web of bare branches in the winter; a spray of stunted yellowish leaves, home to enthusiastically reproductive earwigs, in the summer. Layers of duct tape, generations old, wreathed the windows in a superstitious rather than successful effort to block the winter's sleet and the summer's radiant concrete. And the interior walls, from the cellar to Martin's own garret were slick with damp from the polluted urban inlet that daily ate away at the pilings supporting the older sections of the city.

The water, to Martin, smelt faintly sweet. Corroded. He would have welcomed the egg and sulfur stink of a proper low tide, of healthy mudflats, but he suspected that the bay, a sliver of which he could see from his open window, hadn't hosted organic decay for a century and a half or more.

Nonetheless, Martin was content with his situation. Though his location on the wrong side of the viaduct necessitated three changes of bus—and a perilous sprint across an exit ramp—to reach his place of employment, it also discouraged chance visitors. Martin wrote advertising copy for a fair-trade chocolate company based in a genteelly academic suburb of the financial district. He was very good at what he did. But he shuddered at the thought of it following him home.

In fact, the only aspect of his lifestyle that bothered Martin was the chill that perpetually suffused his neighborhood and, more acutely, his building. In the autumn, when the leaves of the maple trees that flourished in the green area surrounding the chocolate company turned scarlet and golden, reflecting the yellow light of a diminishing yet still warm sun, the pavement fronting his own building was already slick with dirty sludge. The sickly dogwood tree beneath the sodium streetlight stripped of its foliage.

And in the spring, when even the edges of the expressway's off-ramps hosted a sprinkling of battered crocuses, the sleet continued to spit down on him from the moment he left the shelter of the tattered awning half-covering the doorway to the moment he boarded his first bus. His radiator, which came to life in the autumn and ceased to function in the spring via some occult logic and power over which he had no control was always late and always early—Martin, wrapped in blankets, rubbing his hands together, waiting, longing, for the pinging knock and the dry heat that signaled the resurrection of the pipes.

But still, the cold was a small price to pay for the privacy of his location. As much as that cold might bother him now, today, in early March, as he returned home on what had been a warmish afternoon, presaging spring, at the edge of the financial district. Not here, though. Not a breath of it. He shivered, zipped his jacket, pushed his hands into his pockets, and concentrated on avoiding the puddles, frozen solid, that pitted the concrete, as he approached the stairway leading to his front door.

Nodding a greeting at two bluish, emaciated adolescents, he guessed male, one wearing a ski parka but no shoes, the other in thick boots, boxer shorts, and a t-shirt that looked partially eaten, he took hold of the useless iron bannister. Encased in pale ice. Slicker than the stairs themselves. But he made it to the door and forced his key into the lock that was always on the verge of freezing up altogether. He glanced behind him as he entered, wondering whether the boys wanted to follow him into the chilly lobby. They seemed uninterested, and so he let the door close behind him, noting in passing that the scabs on the one, which looked more like the post-mortem work of some graveyard rodent than what he assumed were tracks or abscesses, had spread.

Then he began the long ascent up the spiral staircase to his rooms. Noted the peeling paint. Appreciated the bits and pieces of latex, scattered about the floor, used and discarded. Though the two storeys beneath Martin's rooms were abandoned, the ground floor in its entirety had been a shelter and a needle exchange for as long as anyone in the neighborhood could remember. And the woman who ran it, Bert, welcomed everyone who approached her, regardless of their condition or their ability to function, which meant that in their peregrinations, her visitors more often than not colonized the stairs and the lobby as well as the pavement and the porch.

The majority of these were adolescent boys of the sort he'd seen in the doorway. But there were also a surprising number of middle-aged women. And he'd heard babies wailing more often than he would have expected of a needle exchange—at least before he'd come to live above one.

Martin didn't mind. The eddy of thin, almost transparent waifs and misfits, and the swirl of ragged, wasted bodies forsaken by the world that existed on the other side of the viaduct were another barrier between himself and his life at the chocolate company. Though his colleagues in the genteel suburb certainly approved of the sorts of services that Bert provided, they preferred to hear about those services in the abstract, ideally on public radio, rather than encountering them, and their smell, in person. Martin could be certain that no one would be greeting the blue, scabbed children guarding his doorway prior to dropping in on him unannounced.

But Bert's presence was more to Martin than a means, if a sheepish one, of preserving his privacy. Though not a curious person in general, Martin found himself musing on her whenever his mind was otherwise unoccupied. And sometimes even when it was quite occupied. Looking up from the pages of an uninspiring book. In the two or three minutes before sinking into sleep. While washing a dish. His thoughts, of their own accord, would build up images of the woman who inhabited and permeated the space just beyond the door to his garret.

True, given his location, it would have been difficult to ignore Bert. She and her charges were more an atmosphere than a collection of individuals, seeping into the cracks of the building with the same relentless persistence that the damp cold did in the winter and the equally damp heat did in the summer. Martin couldn't have ignored them even if he'd wanted to.

But he surprised himself by not wanting to ignore them. And he could never quite pinpoint why. Bert herself was a drab and unimpressive person. Closer to elderly than middle aged, she moved her short round body about the building with a pronounced limp. Her most noteworthy characteristic was a large tote bag–a fake, faded Gucci, decades old from some street seller–that was clearly too heavy for her, and which she carried about with her always. He'd once seen her sitting on a curve in the staircase, a sneaker removed, the bag at her side, rubbing a reddened ankle. And though he'd meant to offer her his assistance, he'd been startled into immobility by the deformity of her foot—flat, webbed, and flaking orange, it had struck him as the sort of appendage one might expect to find on an oversized waterfowl.

Though he'd collected himself quickly and offered her his hand, she'd seen his hesitation. Flicking a quick, malicious grin in his direction, she'd risen, hoisted up her bag, and walked briskly, without a limp, further down the staircase. As she'd disappeared, a stray shaft of light had cast an impossible shadow against the wall—the outline of a young girl with cascading hair and flowing dress, absent luggage and trailed by capering imps—before Martin had swallowed, blinked, and continued up to his rooms.

Bert was also immune to the cold that afflicted every other resident in the building. Though she conformed to the unofficial uniform of boots, layers of wool, and down jacket, she apparently did so for reasons of etiquette rather than of necessity. Martin had looked down from his window more than once to see her, in the midst of a January blizzard, sitting on the exterior stairs in nothing more than a nightdress. Barefoot. Awaiting visitors. And, if her serene, contented smile was any indication, none the worse for wear.

But the Bert-related subjects to which Martin's mind most often returned were the stories his neighbors told about her. Undoubtedly exaggerations. It was that sort of neighborhood. Nonetheless, the stories always left him feeling safe and warm. Snug as he drifted off to sleep to the moan of the babies wailing in the stairwell, to the screech of latex ripping outside the door, and to the smell of the toxic bay beyond his window.

His favorite of the Bert legends was her response, so the myth went, to one of the more aggressive visits of the persistent contractors out to buy up property along the waterfront in preparation for the inevitable purification of the bay and sinking of the expressway. For it was a foregone conclusion that one day the expressway would become a tunnel rather than a viaduct, that the sweet smell of chemical waste would become a local attraction, and that the neighborhood would be rebranded a desirable dockside community.

Ordinarily, Bert simply ignored these overtures. But once, so they said, a particularly dangerous example of his type—one with arcane pull and connections to the city's administrative center—refused to retreat. Bullying, healthy, and prosperous, he'd made a nuisance of himself. Until, the neighbors whispered, Bert had invited him indoors to meet her collection of charges. After which, they continued, a day, or two, or perhaps a week, later, the less prominent contractors on the city's lists had found stuffed into the empty shoes they kept in the cupboards of their well-guarded homes the shredded, bleeding pieces of what had once been a bullying, healthy, and prosperous commercial body.

No one had connected the crime to Bert. Few had even considered her. The city had its fair share of maniacal killers, and the creative disposal of bleeding body parts was something of a proud tradition. But the neighbors had nonetheless whispered. And Bert's charges had looked a trifle less blue, a bit less transparent, in the hours following the man's disappearance.

Martin would summon up this story and others similar to it prior to slipping into sleep at the top of the building. Especially in the winter. The rumors made him feel safe.

TODAY, however, something odd was in the air. He could feel it even as he reached the highest landing of the spiral staircase and pushed open the door to his rooms. Which, of course, he never locked. Bert's charges would prevent interlopers from the outside reaching it, and if her guests themselves wanted to inspect his belongings, the flimsy fiberboard wouldn't keep them out, no matter what sort of lock he affixed to it.

He paused on the threshold to examine the space. The radiator was still hissing and pinging, though Martin knew that it was only weeks or days before it went into hibernation. Expelling the thought from his mind, he stepped into the room, heaved the unconscious sigh with which he sloughed off the remnants of his day at the chocolate company, unzipped his jacket, and draped it over the arm of his leatherette recliner. Then he plugged in the electric kettle to heat water for instant soup. While staring out the window at the gathering storm clouds. It would snow tonight. Or sleet. Again.

When he finished his soup, he realized that he was in no mood to sit immobile with a book for the three to four hours that would pass until he might reasonably go to sleep. Unusually, he felt keyed up. Wrong. Twitchy. And so, grabbing his jacket once more, he left his rooms and half jogged down the stairway. A walk would help. By the toxic water. Something to clear his mind.

He was surprised not to encounter skeletal or atrophied shadows as he descended, but not as surprised as he would have been a week ago. There had been a marked decrease in the thronging of Bert's lodgers over the previous days, along with a disquieting increase in rumors that work on removing the viaduct was now, officially, to begin. Come April, said those in the know, the machines would arrive.

Martin, skilled at obliviousness, would under ordinary circumstances have kept himself unaware of these conversations. But their occurrence alongside the thinning of Bert's followers left him uneasy. The two boys were even gone from the entryway when he passed back through the door. Which was thus unguarded. Vulnerable.

He glanced at the anemic dogwood tree, stark and stunted in the circular pool of orange from the streetlight, and then he turned in the direction of the water. Shards of ice spattered his face, whipped up by the chemical breeze from the bay, but he kept his chin level, accepting the onslaught. No one looked twice at him. No one looked at him at all. The streets were empty.

In fact, as he reached the crumbling docks and breakwater, he began to draw the nervous conclusion that the neighborhood had been deserted. No movement behind glowing curtains. No lighted windows. No pedestrians. No furtive economic exchanges in the alleys. Not even the ubiquitous mid-century sedans, lights cut, idling at corners, waiting for custom. No boats in the sludgy inlet.

By the time Martin had reached the unofficial end of the dock—a series of sodden, rotting planks tipped steeply downward toward a collection of pinkish-brown tide pools—he was sufficiently unnerved to wish himself home. Better to hole up insomniac and overly energetic in his rooms with a book that he wouldn't read than wander this bleak, abandoned landscape. At least the radiator was operational.

Therefore, he turned on his heel and, refusing to acknowledge the panicky intake and outflow of his own breath, walked purposefully—but not, he insisted to himself, hysterically—in the direction of his building. Before, giddy with relief, he both caught sight of the exterior stairway and heard the sound of another person. A person sobbing. Human sobbing. One of Bert's waifs—necessarily something else alive in his vicinity.

Aside from the keening that grew in intensity as he neared the stairs, Martin had encountered no evidence of continued habitation anywhere on his side of the viaduct. And thus, though he pitied the source of the wailing, he also felt abstractly comforted. He wasn't–yet–alone.

But at the base of the steps, he paused. The sound was coming not from one of the adolescent boys, or from one of the middle-aged women, or even from Bert herself, but from a child, perhaps six or seven years old, of uncertain gender like so many of Bert's charges, lying face down on the icy concrete stairs. It was clear what had happened. The child had tangled itself in an unraveled thread of its white, cotton nightshirt–the only clothing it wore–and tripped forward over the top step. Martin could see the reddish tinge of a scraped knee and the loose cotton wrapped tightly around one ankle.

He approached the child cautiously, knowing from experience that an angry bite was an entirely likely response to his interest in the situation. But the child merely snuffled and raised its face to his. No damage, as far as Martin could see. The worst of it was the skinned knee and the shock. And the cold. How the child was surviving the spitting ice and the frozen concrete barefoot and wearing light summer cotton he couldn't fathom. But he'd seen worse in the years he'd inhabited his rooms. And the child didn't appear hypothermic. Or even shivering. At the moment.

Without thinking, he held out his jacket to the child, which was gathering itself up into a huddled squat on the top step. He'd neglected to wear the jacket himself as he'd wandered, baffled, across the waterfront. Clutching it in his hand. But the child seemed not to know what to do with it.

And so, once again cautiously, he sat on the top step next to the child and draped the jacket across its shoulders. It didn't protest. But neither did it acknowledge the gesture. Martin, shivering himself now, wrapped his arms across his chest and stared out into the night alongside the child. No one passed. The only sound was the howling of the viaduct.

Eventually, when he could no longer stand the cold, he half turned toward the child. It still seemed to be less affected by the weather than he was. Rubbing its abraded knee, absentmindedly, with the palm of a dirty hand. Scratching the side of one foot with a toenail.

"Would you like to come inside with me?" Martin asked. "Bert might have a bandage for your knee."

For a few seconds, the child remained silent. Then it stood and offered Martin its hand. Martin stood as well, awkwardly took the hand, and walked to the door. With clumsy inexperience, he managed to twist the key in the lock with his one free hand and push open the door with his shoulder.

But the moment they entered the lobby, he knew that something was wrong. The door to

Bert's collection of residential rooms was half open, swinging slightly, as though abandoned only moments before. And though he pushed at the knob half-heartedly, opening the door wide—gratefully releasing the child's hand, which was ice cold and had left his fingers numb—he knew what he would find. The ground floor was abandoned. No furniture. No people. A few scraps of paper, scattered cardboard boxes, and piles of ragged clothing. Latex. Empty.

The child, which had followed a few steps behind him, took in the abandoned rooms with wide, frightened eyes. Then its face began to crumple. Martin, appalled, knelt in front of it and pulled it into an awkward embrace. Then, worried that he might be frightening it further—and shocked by the painful chill of its face against his chest—he stood. A bit too hurriedly.

"Would you like to come upstairs with me?" he offered, uncertain as to what the normal procedure was under these circumstances. "I may be able to find out what happened to Bert." Though how he would do that he had no idea. He couldn't keep himself from chattering.

The child stared up at him, silent and wide-eyed.

"I—I won't hurt you," he said, realizing as soon as the words were out of his mouth that he was sounding increasingly like a predator.

He forced himself to stop. More embarrassed now than anxious or horrified. The child nodded and held out its hand once more. Steeling himself against its painfully frigid skin, he took its hand and they walked slowly and carefully up the spiral stairs to his garret.

When they reached his rooms, the radiator had been cut off. The dry heat had given way to the damp cold that announced the building's reluctant shift toward spring. He glanced down at the child, worried, but it failed to react to the dropping temperature of the room. Instead, casting a solemn glance at Martin's sparse furniture, it appropriated the leatherette armchair and curled itself into a ball.

"Would you like something to eat?" Martin closed the door and gazed about the space as well, willing something other than instant soup to materialize.

Then, feeling foolish, he crossed to the corner where he kept the crates of chocolate forced on him by his employers. Though most of it tasted of chalk or was infused with red pepper, bacon, or quinoa, he knew they also made a contemptuous plain milk chocolate for customers who didn't know better. Unearthing one, he extracted it from the crate and turned toward the child.

But he was too late. The child was asleep, breathing deeply. After a perplexed moment, Martin placed the chocolate on a collapsible table to the side of the armchair, visible to and in reach of his guest, spread a blanket over the small, tightly coiled form, and wandered in the direction of the alcove where he kept his single bed.

IT took Martin less than fifteen minutes of twisting himself up in his bedclothes and shivering against the precipitously dropping temperatures—worse than he'd ever experienced in March—to know that he wouldn't sleep that night. He was tormented by what had become of Bert and her people. Sickened by the thought that he and the child were alone in the neighborhood, separated entirely from the life of the city by the viaduct.

Sitting up in bed, he pulled his boots on over the three pairs of socks he'd worn against the cold, threw his own wool blanket over his shoulders, and returned to the living area. There was a sheet of paper-thin ice covering the child in the leatherette recliner. And the air surrounding the chair felt arctic. But the child was still breathing steadily, deeply asleep, its cheeks pink and its feet kicked free of the blanket.

Martin stared down at it for a few seconds and then made his way to the staircase. Descending was easy, if slippery, in the absence of twitching or semi-reclined bodies. And he was pleased to note when he flicked on the light in Bert's residence that though the radiators were gone, electricity continued to flow to the building. A bare bulb on a string cast a glaring white blaze over the contents of the room. Though these contents, he reconfirmed, were paltry.

Nonetheless, Martin meant to examine them with care. If he could find a clue as to where Bert had gone, he'd be in a position to contact her concerning the child. Otherwise, he'd be forced to call the police–an unhealthy move, he intuited, for either Bert or her charges. He began with the small heap of clothing at the far corner of the room.

Which took him less than a minute to analyze. The ragged leavings of the missing contractor. A few spots of blood. He'd suspected as much and, disappointed more than disgusted, he moved on to a more promising cardboard box on the other side of the space. He could see from where he stood that it was packed with papers. Official-feeling papers. Lowering himself beside it, he leaned against the wall and rubbed his hands together to warm them.

Then, with an inward sigh, he pulled out the first file. Skimmed it quickly. Wrinkled his forehead. Read the next. And the next. He was three quarters through the box, squeamishly handling what were now aged, tissue-thin sheets of the stuff, before he gave up and stopped. The box was full of miscarriage discharge papers. Certificates of miscarriage. Hundreds of them. Stretching back more than a century. A box full of dead–never alive–babies. Not helpful. Not to mention disquieting.

He stood and wandered into one of the smaller back rooms. Kicked aside a bent needle and flicked on the light. More boxes. More miscarriages. He left them. The next room contained additional boxes. These, though, documented suicides. Death certificates. Centuries' worth. Creative and painful suicides.

Martin began to feel ill. Determined, however, to give in neither to his nausea nor to his rising panic, he approached the final room. It was completely empty aside from a single small cardboard box, one corner of which had been eaten away by rot or rats. From where he stood, he could see that it contained photographs rather than papers. Potentially promising.

Not quite trusting himself to react calmly, and shivering convulsively in the coldest air he could remember experiencing anywhere, ever, he forced himself to examine the contents of the box. Black and white, color, a few drawings, at least one lithograph, every image was of a desecrated grave. Graves dug up long after burial. Graves never completed. Graves on the wrong side of the churchyard. Blank, mute headstones. Disfigured headstones. Image after image of graves gone wrong. The incompletely dead complementing the incompletely alive from the first room.

Unable now to keep from shuddering with some violence, and noticing that the skin under his fingernails had turned a shocking blue, Martin abandoned his search. There was nothing to find here. And tomorrow morning, he'd bring the child to the police. Call in sick at the chocolate company for the first time since they'd employed him. They'd understand.

He fled the rooms without troubling to turn off the lights. And though the stairway was now as cold as the ground floor had been, he felt ever more relieved as he put vertical distance between himself and the cardboard boxes. Even without the radiator, his own space would feel warm in comparison. Safe.

But when he pushed open his door and nearly threw himself across the threshold, he discovered Bert herself sitting in his recliner. Rubbing a sore foot. The child resting in her lap, still solemn, holding the chocolate bar, but not eating it. The tote bag, enormous and vibrating, was placed on the floor beside the chair. Martin swallowed and closed the door.

"You're a kind man," Bert announced more to the room at large than to Martin.

He blinked. "The child–"

"Safe and sound," Bert said. "Back where she belongs."

A girl, then. Martin nodded. "You've left? I mean–that is–you're all leaving?" He didn't want to sound as bereft as he felt.

"Hmm." Bert placed the child, still wearing only the cotton nightshirt, on the ground beside her. Stood. Lifted the tote bag over her shoulder. "Expressway's going underground. Time to go."

"So I've heard." He stared at her right foot, broader and flatter than it had been even with the shoe off. And then he stared at her bag. It was doing more than vibrating. It was bulging in and out, its sides straining, emitting an impatient scrabbling sound. He could see what looked like fur or hair shifting about at the opening. As though she were transporting cats. Or weasels.

She smiled, less malicious this time, and re-secured the opening of the bag. The roiling subsided somewhat but didn't cease altogether. "You ought to leave as well."

"I've nowhere to go." He cursed himself for sounding plaintive. Not his intention. "That is—"

"You've got the whole world, Martin."

She nodded at him, took the girl's hand, and led her out the door. A few seconds after they'd cleared the threshold, the radiator announced its return to life with an ear-shattering series of knocks, a ping, and a hiss of burnt, dry air.

Relieved, Martin draped his blanket over the arm of the leatherette chair and approached the ancient coils. Holding his hands above the escaping heat, he glanced, half-interested, out the window. Bert and the girl had exited the building and were lit up by the orange of the sodium light.

Only partially registering what was happening, he watched as Bert stopped, placed the fake Gucci tote on the pavement and spread it open in front of the girl. The girl, still solemn, placed one foot and then, impossibly, the other into the bag. With a wriggle, she compressed herself further down into the tote until only the top of her head was visible. Bert then placed the flat of her own hand on the girl's matted hair and shoved her the rest of the way inside. After which, re-securing the top, she hefted it over her shoulder and disappeared into the darkness.

He noticed, irrelevantly, that the dogwood had leafed out. He'd missed the moment. Again.

Then, turning back to the room, he saw that Bert—or possibly the girl—had left a penny on the collapsible table. Absentminded, he collected it and dropped it into the pocket of his jacket. He could always use spare change.

Frost

THE first week of April was too early to ride a bike comfortably to work, but Yuki liked to set an example for her employees. The chocolate company that she and her husband had built from the ground up was a clean, ecological, fair-trade organization, and its spotless branding was crucial to its not insignificant success. Yuki and her husband encouraged their workers to conform to the brand identity. Walk, jog, bike, or–if they must–make use of public transport. Leave a small footprint.

Besides which, a car park would have blocked the view of their small-batch process, visible through towering glass windows installed at ground level on three of the four sides of the factory they'd repurposed for their needs. A factory that now enhanced, rather than blighting, the green space that the city, in a similar moment of inspiration, had erected two decades earlier over the defunct remains of what had once been a thriving Edwardian industrial area. The park and the factory complemented one another—as did the needs of Yuki and those of the city.

The maple trees surrounding the factory, for example, were only a touch more twisted, a trifle more colorful, on their diet of nineteenth-century chemical waste than they ought to be. And the mellow light that suffused the glass, regardless of the season or the time of day, was only a hint too golden. Atmospheric rather than poisonous. A draw for visitors rather than a stain on the city's history.

And indeed, it had become fashionable in recent months for tourists strolling the space—which represented, now, a bridge rather than a gulf between the financial district and the University campus where Yuki's husband had once taught—to pause and watch the chocolate being produced. While Yuki herself, anxious, invisible behind the opaque fourth wall, labored inside, monitoring Yelp and Wikipedia for evidence that their company was flourishing in the proper direction. Growing atmospherically, rather than poisonously.

Proper growth was important because Yuki had gambled quite a lot on the continuing health of the company. When her husband had won the MacArthur Grant three years previously—a welcome public acknowledgment of his groundbreaking intersectional work on endangered honey bees and systemic urban poverty—they'd faced a life-transforming choice. Either use the money to launch an expanded research project or use it as partial funding for an entirely new exploration of entrepreneurship. Throwing over the bees and the poor people had been a difficult decision—but one that had proved profitable within six months of raising their seed capital. Their building, a portal between the world of finance and the life of the mind, had become, by the end of their first year in business, an institution; and their chocolate was now an international phenomenon. Yuki, who was by no means the sort of person to think small, had herself been astonished by their success.

NONETHELESS, she was now cursing under her breath as she locked her bike onto the stand at the edge of the University campus. Feeling burdened and deflated. She'd skidded on an invisible patch of frost and ice as she'd braked, and her ankle throbbed from having fought to keep her balance. A demeaning accident. Some watching graduate student had even laughed.

More than that, though, she was brooding on the setback that her company was facing for the first time since its inauguration. A setback, moreover, that should never have struck them to begin with. Not merely an accident. An oversight.

It had all started two weeks ago, when their advertising copy editor—a man who had been pleased to work for a fraction of the salary they paid their other, largely ornamental, employees—had quit. A financial windfall, he'd told her. And then, mumbling something about moving someplace warm, he'd disappeared into the ether.

Gone before Yuki had even understood his importance to their business model.

But he'd been such a nonentity, she raged to herself as she limped away from the bike rack, so lacking in brand enthusiasm, she'd scarcely been aware of his work when he'd been on the payroll. Besides which, she believed he rode the bus. And surely their chocolate sold itself?

Apparently not. Within three days of his disappearance, their sales had plummeted. A day or two after that, the tourists gathered beyond the glass front of their factory had begun to appear cynical about, rather than enchanted by, its small-batch transparency. By the colorful maple trees. The yellow light.

And then, catastrophe had struck. The next evening, all of their Yelp pages–followed quickly by Wikipedia–had been inundated with snide hints that their trade negotiations with the governments ruling the regions from which they sourced their material were less fair than the company's copy had been in the habit of claiming. Yuki's lips thinned at the thought–what were they supposed to do? Grow the plants here? Last year, April had arrived on the heels of a blizzard that had dropped two feet of the snow on the city. Chocolate, as any reasonable customer would accept, demanded that one occasionally look the other way.

Frustrated, she knocked a chunk of frost from the bottom of her cleated shoe; winced as her ankle twinged; and then continued hobbling.

Fretting. Noticing out of a corner of her eye that the prints her shoes left in the frost were fainter than usual. The cleat marks less visible. Then she pushed the haphazard thought away.

She paused to purchase herself a cup of coffee from the espresso stand she'd patronized for longer than she and her husband had owned the company. A campus legend. Rummaged about in her public radio shoulder bag for the travel mug she carried for that purpose. Paid. Tipped extravagantly. Crossed the chaotic square toward the secondary branch of the University bookstore and the diagonal street beyond it that led in the direction of the green space and the factory.

As she walked, she tried to disregard the ungainly proportions of the intersection–less a square than a pulsating amoeboid blob radiating aimless avenues in futile and counterproductive directions. Years ago, when she'd first lived in the city, she'd repeatedly taken incorrect diagonals, walking miles away from her destination before realizing her error. And then backtracking. Minutes, sometimes hours, late to whatever appointment she'd optimistically scheduled. Unable to understand how she'd followed the wrong path in the first place.

For the roads slicing through her husband's campus were neither intricate nor complicated. Nor were they the winding alleyways of her youth. Nothing about them was medieval or charming. Or labyrinthine. Labyrinthine she could handle. No, the roads crossing the square were straight, aggressive thoroughfares that, nonetheless, for reasons she could never quite divine, always led in the wrong direction.

She concentrated even now on choosing the proper street as she sipped her coffee and ignored her ankle. Less anxious than she'd been in the early days. She'd learned from experience that in the winter and the spring, at least, she could follow her own frosted footprints back again should she enter unfamiliar territory. She wrinkled her forehead as she glanced down at her shoes once more. The frost today must be colder than it felt. Her cleats were scarcely making a dent as she trudged across the square.

Then, embittered by the accumulating vexations of the morning, she terminated the thought and stopped mid-stride. The vagrant was back. Huddled up in a blanket outside the glass doors of the bookstore. Warmed, perhaps, by the gusts of heated air that escaped the building as students pushed in and out. Waiting for her.

She resumed walking. Obviously, he wasn't waiting for her. He was doing his job just as she was attempting to do hers. But she nevertheless felt an unpleasant connection to the man, and whenever she encountered him, she became irrationally certain that ill luck would follow. If nothing else, she loathed the drop in temperature—psychosomatic on her part, no doubt—that she sensed in his vicinity. Even in the middle of August, he carried with him the quivering air of a frosty spring day.

In fact, her distaste for the man had begun the August before, in the midst of what had been a heat wave everywhere else. She'd been on her way to work, just as she was now, and she'd glanced down at him—inadvertently, accidentally—as she'd passed the bookstore and sensed the chill. At which point, two entirely disconnected thoughts had struck her. The first was that the plastic water bottle he kept with him was an environmental catastrophe—that someone really ought to find him something in stainless steel. And the second was that he was the most beautiful man she'd ever seen.

Both thoughts had left her perturbed. The first because she wasn't certain that concerning herself with the state of the water bottle rather than with the state of the man was an appropriate response to the situation. She liked to think of herself as effortlessly ethical, and her reaction felt to her a touch discordant. She resented him for provoking it in her.

As for the second—well, it was absurd. Her husband was beautiful. No one else. Ever. A clean, lithe intellectual, he ran marathons. He was healthy. Sound in mind and body. Whereas this figure crouching on the pavement in front of the bookstore was, at best, a cautionary tale. A spot of corruption. Despite his extraordinary eyes—

In the split second that these musings had all shoved themselves simultaneously into her frontal lobe, Yuki had also, to her disgust, intuited that the man himself had followed her thinking as clearly as if she'd spoken aloud. He'd neither commented nor smiled. Nor did he smirk or attempt contact with her—his beautiful, blank face remained as blank as ever. But she knew that he knew. And she was mortified.

Most distressing of all, though—more than any of the other horrors of that day in August—she'd felt, ever since that moment, compelled to notice him. Supremely, uncomfortably aware of him. Beyond the espresso stand. On the other side of the square.

She refused, of course, to change her route, which would have represented an acknowledgment of her discomfort. But this refusal only meant that her dread upon approaching the spot had become a daily occurrence. A daily torment.

Granted, he wasn't always there. But he often was. And she could count on seeing him at least two or three times in a week. Always wrapped in the same beige wool blanket. Always the same smooth black hair. The same deep eyes under the same brows like raven's wings. The same sculpted features. The same smooth, opaque skin. The same hint of muscled shoulders—

It wasn't until early October that she realized he wasn't alone. In the folds of the blanket, she was startled one morning to notice, he also kept an infant. An infant as beautiful as the man himself. Equally blank. Unearthly. Calm. She wondered how he'd managed to hide the child from Social Services. But mostly, she shuddered.

Because Yuki hated babies. Not vocally, of course. She certainly never proselytized. Most of her friends and her husband's colleagues had reproduced, and she believed that she played the role of childless auntie as well as could be expected. But in the abstract, babies left her nauseated. When she considered the situation, it thus failed to surprise her that the disconcerting figure who ruined her ride and walk to work at least sixty percent of the time also sported a child.

And once she'd noted the baby, it took her very little time to detect other abnormalities in his behavior. For example, the quiet requests he made of various passers-by were neither for help nor for work. Nor did he ask for money. Or food. Rather, once she began listening—which she chided herself for doing; best remain uninvolved—she determined that he was asking those who neared him to hold the baby. To comfort the baby. To lift the baby. The realization left her queasy.

After a few surreptitious glances at the pedestrians surrounding her on the street, she additionally concluded that, aside from herself, people weren't ignoring the man so much as failing to see him. Their indifference to his request was too natural, too unstudied, to be anything but a genuine inability to hear what he was saying. Yuki alone *ignored* him. And she did so with decreasing adequacy. The problem, she ranted to herself, was simply that he was just so beauti—

She had come to this conclusion—that only she truly saw the man—sometime in early January, as she tramped through drifts of snow after parking her Porsche SUV sufficiently distant from the green space that her employees wouldn't see it. And since then, her brushes with him had been characterized as much by fear as by irritation. Something was wrong with him. With the baby. With the situation. And she alone could sense it.

Standing in the middle of the square, she gazed balefully across the intersection. Then, fighting her limp, she squared her shoulders and sipped her coffee. She had more important issues to occupy herself than her irrational aversion to a homeless man and his child. For once, she really would fail to notice him. Her mind otherwise occupied.

She ran over the list of the day's duties in her head as she walked. First, she meant to find herself one or two of what her husband liked to call Parasocial Ideologues. Influencers. Whatever. Or ten. She'd pass the earliest part of the day concentrating on that. A resource infinitely more effective to propping up the company's hobbled brand than some drab writer hidden in a corner hatching slogans. And she'd likely get on with the Parasocial Ideologues better than she had with whatever his name had been. Bright, brave, extroverted people. She might even make a few friends.

Insufficient nerve was his problem, she muttered, failing to move on to the second item on her list as she reached the other side of the square. Fleeing the cold, indeed. She limped past the vagrant, defiant, casting a careless glance at the baby. Frost was bracing. Invigorating. And his eyes were like pools of dark water—

She glared at the ground and kept walking.

YUKI spent the day engaged in damage control because the faint hints of corporate impropriety that had emerged on a few scattered websites the previous week had now blossomed into a full-blown scandal. Overwhelming her morning. And not a single one of the Parasocial Ideologues she approached was interested in tainting his or her brand with Yuki's. A humiliating turn of events, though she appreciated their position. She understood, from gloating competitors, that there were at this point even memes involved in the company's disgrace. Though she refused to seek them out.

Worse, by late afternoon, protesters had begun to deface the glass windows encircling the ground floor of the factory. Thus far, they hadn't become violent—contenting themselves with tracing rude images in the frost that had unaccountably accumulated on the outside of the heated building. But their muddy footprints, churning up the ground, had made the approach to the doorways treacherous. Or, at least, unpleasant. She sent her employees home an hour early, concerned about their safety (and litigation). She also sent her husband home when he began soliloquizing wistfully about bees and poverty. Rage at his fecklessness was not a helpful emotion under the present circumstances.

Then she sat at her desk and held her head in her hands. It was all happening so quickly. As though they'd been cursed by some supernatural affliction. But Yuki wasn't the sort to buckle under pressure, and she was confident that she would stem the onslaught of negative publicity. She was a talented and resourceful person. She would work all night, if necessary.

Which she did. And as the muffled chimes of the public clock in the financial district struck three the next morning, she was beginning to feel a hint of optimism. The tide, she sensed, was turning. Tomorrow, she'd be fighting back.

And so, switching off the lamp on her desk, she rose, stretched, and retrieved her coat from the empty chair into which she'd dumped it that morning. She would return home, sleep for a few hours, and then complete her counter attack the next day. The walk and ride through the cold, empty streets would help to clear her mind. Relax her taut nerves.

When she passed through the front doors of the factory building, she frowned down at the muddy troughs surrounding it. Frothed up by the protestors and the touristic spectators during the day's excitement, they were now frozen into solid furrows. Unattractive. Far from green. Then, her frown becoming a sneer, she approached the nearest disfigured window: "Whats behind the fourth wall!"

She stared at the tag. The punctuation was incorrect. And the unflattering image of her husband doing something inappropriate with a bee was simply unfair. Balancing herself on a hummock of mud, she rubbed her palm against the etched frost. But she couldn't erase it. If anything, the window felt warmer to her than her hand did.

She hopped off her perch and shrugged. She'd hire someone tomorrow to spray it with antifreeze. Replace the glass with the work of some local artist. Perhaps coopt the vandals themselves. They'd like that. Or, at least, they'd like the money.

The mud was solid enough that the weight of her cleated shoes scarcely scraped it as she worked her way back to the road. And as she strode down the thoroughfare in the direction of the square, she left only the faintest trace of a print. But she didn't notice. Buoyed up by her coming victory over the negative press, she closed her eyes and instead took deep, extravagant breaths of the sharp air. The empty night was her favorite time to be out in the city. And the purity of the atmosphere tonight, this night, was sufficiently intense to sting her eyelids and lungs. A rare pleasure.

She opened her eyes only when she reached the closed branch of the University bookstore. Lurching to a halt. The intersection was empty. The pavement was deserted. No one was about.

No one was about.

No one was about except for the vagrant, who was standing in the middle of the intersection, holding his infant, and staring at her. He'd pushed back the blanket from his shoulders, and Yuki could see what he hid beneath it.

Nothing.

Or, he was naked. Far from nothing. Notwithstanding her astonishment and growing terror, she noted that he was as physically perfect in the parts she'd never seen as he was physically perfect in every other way. Her breathing, involuntarily, became short and shallow.

Then she damped down the terror. She had stopped between ten and fifteen feet away from the man, and she could sense from where she stood that he meant her no harm. And even had he tried to attack her, she could easily defend herself. She felt in no physical danger.

But the spectacle was disconcerting enough that in a parody of her ineffectively feigned daylight indifference, she dropped her eyes, ignored his presence, and stalked away from the square in the direction of her bike. She'd treat herself to a large glass of bourbon when she made it home. Sleep, at this point, was less important to her than dulling her senses. She didn't even want to think about the dreams that this latest encounter with the vagrant would stimulate.

It took her close to twenty-five minutes of incensed walking to realize that she'd taken the wrong diagonal. She did recognize the neighborhood she'd entered. But the dark, residential buildings were not those she wanted. She'd made another stupid error. Fuming, she turned on her heel and followed her footsteps—nearly invisible on the hard frost—back in the direction of the square.

When she reached the intersection, the man was still there. Still calm. Still holding the baby. Still watching her. Still naked. And so, coloring once again, she found the road she wanted and began jogging in the direction of her bike.

Ten minutes later, she knew she'd made another mistake. At this rate, it would be dawn before she found her front door. Curious as to the time, in fact, she extracted her phone from her coat pocket, thinking she might make use of the navigation app as well—no graduate students at this hour to mock her—and checked the screen. No satellite. No time. No battery.

It was unlike her to forget to charge the phone, but she forgave herself. The past two weeks had been chaotic. She zipped the phone into her pocket and retraced her steps. Metaphorically. Because there were now no footprints at all to follow. But the road was straight and simple. At least, it was straight and simple going toward the square. Away from the square was proving to be more of a challenge.

The man was still standing in the intersection. She ignored him and chose what she was certain must be the proper thoroughfare. It wasn't. Refusing to acknowledge defeat, Yuki systematically tested every road leading out of the square—more roads than could possibly have intersected it; more hours than were left in the night. But she remained stranded.

Until finally, as the sun should have been rising but wasn't, she returned to her position opposite the vagrant. Accepting failure. He hadn't changed his position in all the hours she'd been walking except to turn in her direction as she'd struggled in and out of the square. Now, once more, he stood naked and beautiful, the blanket draped over his shoulders, facing her.

Less gracious than she wanted to be, Yuki approached the man. Halted in the middle of the intersection, observing him. She was close enough to have to look up into his face. Cold air sloughing off his perfect skin in almost visible torrents. She shivered.

Then, steeling herself, she spoke. "I think," she said to him, "that I'm lost. Can you help?"

He gazed down at her for a few seconds before lifting the infant. "Hold this."

She blinked, considering. And then she extended her hands. If comforting the child was his price, she would pay it. She'd been forced to touch the babies of countless friends and acquaintances before—this couldn't be any worse. And perhaps it would last only a few seconds as he divulged whatever arcane instructions she sensed he alone possessed.

After a brief nod, he settled the baby into her arms. Instinctively, she held it closer to her. The baby was as naked as the man, and the weather was glacial. But rather than speaking further, explaining her situation, or even pointing her toward a likely path, the man simply turned his back on her, dropped the blanket to the frosted concrete, and walked away. Completely naked now.

Yuki was so stunned by the man's behavior that she remained frozen in place for several seconds as he departed. And when she came to herself and attempted to follow him, at least in order to return his baby, two further observations presented themselves to her. The first was that his footprints, which had initially been invisible, and then as faint as her own, had grown stronger and deeper the further away from her he'd walked. Though distant, they were close to luminescent at the edge of the square.

The second was that with every stride he took, the baby grew heavier. It was already more than she could comfortably support in her two hands. Panicky, she considered for a few seconds leaving it in the heap of blanket on the concrete, but she couldn't bring herself to abandon it in the middle of the street. And by the time she had shifted it into a convenient, if not relaxed, position, the man had vanished. All that remained of him was a set of pronounced footprints, vivid as they left the intersection.

As she debated the utility of following the trail he'd left, the stars began to dim, and the black sky lightened into a grey dawn. Relieved at the resumption, at least, of time, she decided to let the homeless man go. He couldn't help her. And it might even be irresponsible to place a vulnerable infant into his care.

Yuki knew that the square would fill with people once the sun had risen, and she'd easily find among them both someone to help her locate her bike and someone with a solution to the baby problem. In the meantime, she'd shelter herself in the lee of the bookstore. Mentally enumerating, once more, the duties that faced her that day.

Glancing with satisfaction at the line of reddish sunlight at edge of the easternmost of the thoroughfares, she gathered up the blanket, wrapped it around her shoulders for additional warmth, and approached the familiar glass doors. Then she huddled down beside them in the blanket, cuddling the cold, heavy baby against her chest. In her relief at the increasing light, she closed her eyes and allowed herself to drift into a brief sleep.

She must have slept for longer than she'd intended, however, because when she was awakened by a gust of warm air—uncomfortably warm air—exhaled from the bookstore's open doorway, the square was packed with afternoon pedestrians. After her initial confusion, she smiled and rubbed her eyes. All the better. More potential solutions to the difficulties that had presented themselves to her.

But as she politely addressed those who passed, busy and preoccupied, no one answered. No one even noticed her. For a brief moment, she was consumed by rage at their treatment of her.

Before, almost simultaneously, she realized how she must appear to them, and she flushed. The blanket, the baby, and the pavement were hardly invitations to engage in conversation.

First off, therefore, she'd stand.

She couldn't stand.

The baby, like some seventeenth-century cannonball, kept her anchored in place at the edge of the bookstore's entrance. Blocking off the circulation to her legs, and she could only imagine what else. Dead weight.

Genuinely angry now, and not caring all that much what became of the infant, she rolled it off of her lap and away from the edge of the blanket. It gazed up at her from the concrete, blank, beautiful, and calm. She wished briefly that it were dead as well as catatonic, but then she decided that she didn't feel strongly enough about it to want it gone. Dismissed the thought as unimportant.

The baby no longer affixing her to the ground, she stood and shrugged off the blanket. Leaving herself, she realized after a split second of astonished dismay, entirely naked. Shocked—though no one passing appeared to notice—she hastily gathered up the beige wool and covered herself with it. Confused as to how she felt no cold. How, in fact, she felt nothing at all of the air on her skin. Aside from the unpleasant heat of the bookstore. She hunkered down against the less hot—in fact, refreshingly cool—window.

Then she experimented with pressing her hand against the exterior glass. No print. No condensation. All she left was a faint, negligible outline of frost.

After a few further seconds, another idea occurred to her, and she peered down at her feet. She'd been crossing back and forth over the muddy gutter fronting the establishment, and her feet ought to have been caked with dirt. The quick glance confirmed, however, that they weren't. Her skin was immaculate. Clean and perfect.

It took her a few additional seconds to appreciate the implications of that last observation. And then, in a moment of inspiration, it came to her. No footprint. She was leaving no footprint at all.

Gathering up the baby, Yuki gazed down into its empty face. Beautiful and vacant. Just as a baby ought to be. Her baby. Her footprint. She relaxed and watched the people passing by. Content. Uninterested, after all, in eliciting attention from any of them.

Melt

WHAT are you doing?"

Malia watched, confused but not very interested, as Pelleas took an axe to his latest unfinished project.

"I'm destroying it."

"Why?"

"It's shit."

She tilted her head. A strand of silken, perfectly-styled hair briefly obscured one blue eye. As far as she was concerned, all of Pelleas's work was shit. But expressing her opinion wouldn't help the situation. Her boredom grew.

She considered, not for the first time, giving up on Pelleas and finding herself another artist. He wasn't her first. He wasn't even her tenth. And it was close to two years now since he'd won the award for that installation.

"Cake Walk." An invitation to the City Museum's donors to remove their architectural and irreplaceable footwear before walking barefoot through a thirty-foot square of yellow sheet cake upon entering the Museum's annual summer gala.

Small rosettes of pink frosting at each corner. Paper plates for those who'd wanted them.

The tent enclosing Cake Walk had been installed on the night of the party to the side of the grand stairway leading up to the central galleries. Optional, obviously. But no one had wanted to appear lacking in whimsy. And Malia herself, attending alone, between artists, had adored it. Squelching up the marble stairs in her diamond-studded Rene Caovilla slingbacks, slick with frosting, she had vowed to add its creator to her collection.

Her desire had become close to unbearable as hours had passed, and the curious fug of damp feet and vanilla cake gone wrong that hung over the party had increased in intensity, the floors ever more treacherous as bits of frosting continued to spill from donors' shoes, until the last of the guests had departed. Just a hint earlier than usual. Occasionally, on the rare days she ventured into the Museum without an invitation that cost the same as a car, she believed that she could still catch a hint of rancid cake in the air.

And then ultimately, when the critics, after teetering between disgust and applause for a tense three or four hours following the closing of the Museum's doors, had the next morning crowned Pelleas the artistic genius of the moment, she'd made her move. Before any of her competitors had recovered from the previous night's alcohol poisoning. She was beneath the window of his studio-loft at the edge of the Malaysian district just as the sun was rising.

Not that Pelleas had been a difficult conquest. Dazzled by his overnight success and celebrity, he'd fallen to Malia's formulaic technique within seconds of opening his padlocked door to her. She was the fantasy of every artist without a great deal of imagination who had ever taken a Greyhound bus to pursue his creative dream in the nearest fashionable city. She was perfect.

Because, as Pelleas soon discovered, Malia was more than just rich. True, her family owned one of the more flamboyantly unscrupulous of the big five pharmaceutical companies, meaning that she could easily sacrifice a truckload of delicate, gem-encrusted shoes to frosted vanilla sheet cake without the tiniest stab of regret. And when she mentioned her "collection" to her father, he really didn't care one way or the other whether she was referring to art or to artists. She was his excruciatingly well-funded baby.

More than that, though, she was intelligent. The vanity Ph.D. that she was completing in "Translation Studies with Particular Reference to the Poetic Edda, Inclusive of Glossary" at the nearby University, for example, was a good sixty percent her own work. And when she periodically attended a seminar or a talk by a visiting scholar, she enjoyed infuriating her impoverished counterparts in the graduate program by asking not entirely stupid questions. She was the real thing— and she enjoyed it.

At the moment, however, she was leaning against one of the many rusted iron shafts that partially supported the bare ceiling of Pelleas's loft, watching as he ripped apart a large, anthropomorphic sea otter made of pink painted Styrofoam. Though it didn't rip so much as bounce slowly about the space like an affronted balloon. She peered down at her fingernails, bitten to the quick–she liked to let people think she dabbled in piano–and then back up at Pelleas, enraged now, battling the otter with his axe. She'd keep him, she decided, for a few more weeks. The scene with the Styrofoam was entertaining her.

"Take me out to dinner."

He stopped hacking, leaving the sea otter largely unscathed, and looked up at her, panting. "What?"

"I'm hungry. Take me out to dinner. There's a new Malaysian place."

He let the axe drop to the floor. "It's the Malaysian district, Malia."

"You see?"

Habituated to obedience, Pelleas ran a hand through his sweaty hair, grabbed a jacket, and stalked to the steel door. Rolled it up and beckoned her through. He could eat.

MAYBE a month or so ago," Malia was saying, "in the square. You remember how cold it still was? It was a few days after Jen and I saw that angry corporate lady skidding out on her bike." She smiled at the memory.

Pelleas picked at his food, not listening. His own dish contained unidentifiable bits and pieces of one large fish, in curry, whereas Malia's consisted in a slew of equally unidentifiable tiny fish, also in curry. One was slightly less orange than the other. He squirted something green from a bottle into the bowl and swirled the colors.

"Anyway," she pushed on, "so this creepy homeless woman with a *baby* starts blocking my way into the bookstore every time I'm there. I tried to give her money, but she wouldn't take it. Just kept staring at me. Shoving the baby in my face."

She flicked a miniscule fish into her mouth and kept talking. "So, I asked Andrew–you know, Big Andrew, to take care of her–seriously, she was freaking me out–but he said he couldn't find her. So I went back with him, and she was right there, stoned or high or whatever like always. And I told him–"

She frowned across the table at Pelleas. "You aren't listening."

"Yes, I am." He considered the surface of his bowl. "What's this green stuff?"

She wiped her fingers on her napkin. "Okay, do you know what? What you need is inspiration. And I've got a brilliant idea."

"What is it?"

"Let's go to the Museum tomorrow."

He was sufficiently startled to look up from his food. "I don't go to the Museum." He hadn't been since Cake Walk. Nowadays even the neighborhood depressed him. "I don't want to go to the Museum."

"Not the City Museum," she said. "The Vogel. Downtown. It's intimate. Less daunting."

"It's also empty. Their paintings were all stolen last year in that heist." He frowned down at the brownish edges of the green swirl he'd concocted. "I'm surprised you don't remember."

"No worries. You don't paint." She placed her napkin on the table, indicating that they'd finished. "The atrium is nice. Interesting atmosphere. It will help you recover your, you know, groove, mojo—whatever."

And Pelleas, still trained to obedience, signaled for the bill. "All right."

THEY walked through the hushed, empty lobby of the Vogel—unpopular since the museum's collection had disappeared in one, dramatic airport-novel-like night—at eleven the following morning. The porter, recognizing Malia, waved them into the central gallery without checking their tickets. And Pelleas, looking about him, was surprised that so little had been done to repair what was now thirteen- or fourteen-month-old damage.

He could still see the gouged wood where the thieves had dragged their haul across the floor. He could still see the cracked lenses of the useless cameras affixed to the ceiling. He could still see the dent in the desk where the sole night guard had been neutralized like something out of the Marx Brothers.

And saddened, he shuddered. But this reaction wasn't new. Pelleas had always shuddered upon entering the building, even when it still had its art, because he'd never been able to reconcile the collection with its setting. The two together set his teeth on edge.

Housed in a structure of harrowing bad taste commissioned by one of the city's first industrial magnates, the Vogel Collection affected many of its visitors in this way. On the one hand, there was the mansion itself. Drawing on the late-nineteenth-century fashion for mentally ill Bavarian and Black Forest kitsch, Aloysius Vogel's architects had, under his heavy-handed patronage, raised a wooden palace on the banks of the river responsible for carrying away his factory waste that was nothing more nor less than a massive, menacing, inhabitable cuckoo clock. A monstrosity.

The balustrades lining the façade were not only shaped like towers of psychedelic mushrooms atop swirls of whipped cream, but they were also painted in exuberantly clashing pastels. And gilded. Inside, marginal carving along the dark wood paneling depicted the shocking—especially given its nineteenth-century provenance—misdeeds of countless teetering, leering, minatory woodland gnomes and dwarves. It was a building to raise the hackles. On the hour, everything in it pinged and chimed.

But then, on the other hand, there were the paintings, purchased by Vogel's descendants. These had always been subdued–increasingly subdued, in fact, as Vogel's memory had receded. And thus, in their time, they had been the object of both envy and respect. They weren't in evidence now, of course. Though their ghosts insistently lingered.

Pelleas blinked, bemused, as he gazed up at the empty walls. Discolored where the pictures had hung. Their identifying cards still affixed at eye level.

Malia grinned and took his arm. "Shall we?"

He nodded, and they approached the first stretch of blank wall.

"Monet," she read from the card. "'Charing Cross Bridge, London,'" After a few seconds of silence, they moved on. "Cézanne. 'View of Auvers-sur-Oise."

Malia narrowed her eyes, dropped his arm, and crossed to the other side of the room. "Impressionists bore me. Let's try over here instead."

"I'm not sure Cézanne is really–" Pelleas began as he followed her, feeling uncomfortable. The walls, missing their paintings, were eerie. Distressing. In their own silenced way, they were an atrocity. His stomach quietly began twisting itself into knots.

"Ah," she cried. "This is better. 'Caravaggio. "Nativity with St. Francis and St. Lawrence.'" She tilted her head. "It was big, wasn't it?"

"Malia," he tried again. "This is ghoulish. And there's no one around. I think we ought to go."

"There's not no one around."

To demonstrate, she lifted her chin toward a corner of the room that was darker than it ought to have been in a gallery. Even a gallery with no paintings. Peering up at another blank spot on the wall was someone else. A small, gnome-like man with a pronounced hump on his left shoulder.

Feeling their interest, he turned toward them. Then he bowed slightly and resumed his inspection of the wall. Pelleas began to speak again, but Malia interrupted him, giggling.

"And goodness." She turned toward another figure. "He's enjoying himself. There isn't even anything in front of him to provoke that."

Pelleas glanced in the direction she'd indicated and then quickly looked away. The man, also tiny, also old yet spry, wore an anachronistic hat and an enormous erection. Pelleas could see it—both—even in the dim light, from the other side of the room.

"Let's *go*," he whispered.

"No," Malia persisted, relentless, "I want to see what's got him so excited."

Dragging Pelleas along behind her, she marched across the room. As they neared the tiny man, Pelleas noticed that the floor became faintly damp. Slippery under their feet. Malia slowed at the same time.

"That can't be—" she said.

"Of course not," he snapped. "It's the weather. Spring. It's damp."

"It's May," she said.

"A damp May."

The man, hearing them arguing behind him, turned, raised his hat politely, and left the room. His erection remained prominent and distracting. Pelleas looked behind him and saw that the man with the humped shoulder had also disappeared.

"Malia," he repeated, "I don't like this. I want to go."

"'Landscape with Cottages' by Rembrandt." She was gazing up at the blank wall. "Strange man." She let her eyes fall. And then she grinned at him. "Not Rembrandt."

"Yes," he said. "I followed your meaning."

"The atrium is through here," she continued. "It will calm you." She began walking. "It may even inspire you. More than the pink otter, at any rate."

Irritated, he trotted behind her. Vowing to stay no more than five minutes before returning to his studio. This had been an ill-advised idea.

But when he entered the warm, humid space, Pelleas's mood began, for the first time in months, to lift. The atrium, an addendum to the building by Vogel's descendants, was relaxing. Pleasing. An antidote to the aggression of the remainder of the building. To the gnomes, dwarves, and relentless chimes.

Empty aside from Malia and himself, the room in fact felt almost healing. The translucent roof let in just sufficient light to encourage the palms and the Colocasia to grow. And the rectangular pool at its center, through some trick of the tiles lining it, looked simultaneously pellucid and bottomless. As though one could lose oneself in it, and not regret the loss.

Pelleas found a marble bench at the side of the pool and sat. Malia, uncharacteristically quiet, sat beside him. A few seconds passed silently, and then the sound of a flute began to float across the greenery. Melancholy and not quite tempered.

Malia's head went up. "What's that?"

"I don't know. It's nice, though."

"No, it isn't. It's giving me a headache."

"Oh," he said, pointing to the other side of the pool. "There."

A boy, perhaps fourteen or fifteen years old, ugly but happy, was playing an instrument that resembled a flute but wasn't anything Pelleas had ever seen in a musician's hands. The boy nodded to them both without interrupting his performance, and then he closed his eyes. The tempo picked up a tick.

"I don't think that's allowed in here," Malia muttered.

"Maybe they've hired him." Pelleas was impressed by the deceptive restraint of the boy's playing. He wondered whether one might buy a recording of it from the gift shop.

Malia stood. "I don't like it. I'm leaving."

Pelleas looked up at her. "Give me five minutes, would you? I'll meet you outside. I want to hear how it ends."

"Stay as long as you like," she replied. "I've got a seminar. I'm glad you're enjoying it."

Pelleas knew better than to try to decipher her tone. Malia always meant precisely what she said. She didn't care enough about him to try to manipulate him. To stoop to passive aggression.

"Okay. See you tonight?"

"Fine—" she began. Then her eyes wide, she stared down at the pool. "Jesus. What was that?"

"What?"

"There's something in the water. A snake or something." She put her hand over her mouth. "Something big. I saw it."

"I didn't see anything."

"Like a serpent with a huge red eye—" She caught herself and laughed. "Great. Next I'll be attacking a Styrofoam otter with an axe. You're contagious, sweetie."

He smiled up at her. "I'll buy you something from the gift shop on my way out."

"I'd be desolate if you didn't." Kissing his cheek, she returned to the archway. Stepping carefully to keep her balance on the now saturated tiles. The room felt more than humid now. Steaming. For the plants, presumably.

Before she passed out of the atrium, she turned and frowned down again at the trail she'd left through the condensed water.

"That's odd," she said after a few seconds. "Do my footprints seem smaller to you?"

"You've got small feet, Malia. I, if anyone, ought to know."

"Huh." Dissatisfied. "Weird."

But then, without pursuing the thought further, she left the room.

Pelleas sat quietly for a good ten minutes after Malia had left, savoring the heat and the damp. The boy never ceased his playing, and indeed his song seemed to be increasing in complexity as time passed. Eventually, however, curious about the pool, Pelleas rose and approached the edge of the water.

He could understand how Malia had imagined a creature living in it. The bottom was effectively invisible. The liquid both clear and dark. He himself couldn't be certain that he didn't see a twisted muscular tail or a fin, some impossible fish, sliding beneath the surface as he stared into it. Then, shaking his head to rid it of the vision, he dipped his fingertips into the pool–though he knew he wasn't supposed to–and rubbed his temples with the water. Healing.

As he stood to leave the atrium and find the gift shop, he noticed a final exhibit–or the remains of an exhibit–that he'd not yet inspected. At the far end of the atrium, it looked more like a reliquary on a stand than a deliberate display but, dutifully, he approached it with mild interest.

When he saw what the clear, rock-crystal box positioned on a waist-high marble pedestal contained, though, he drew in his breath. It was incomprehensible that the thieves would have made off with what he'd always considered second-rate works by tired and over-rated artists while leaving this exquisite object untouched. Unmolested.

And the object was exquisite. A red gemstone the size of his fist–ignorant, he would have guessed a ruby, but he suspected a less common material–it not only drew his attention but held him rapt. He couldn't keep from staring at it.

Moreover, as he did so, the music from the flute–an aural manifestation of the gemstone itself–swelled and insinuated itself into his mind. Until he could feel and hear nothing else. Nothing, that is, aside from the surface of the pool becoming agitated, waves rippling and then rising on it, merging with the wet of the room. In fact, it was only his curiosity about the state of the pool that finally freed his eyes from the stone.

But when he looked behind him, the pool was calm. The room empty. Even the music was gone. The boy had withdrawn to the place from which he'd emerged. The only evidence of Pelleas's experience was the wet. Not only were the benches, the floor, and the plants dripping as though they'd been submerged under a tidal swell, but his own clothing was soaked through. Anyone seeing him would think he'd fallen into the pool rather than simply resting beside it.

Unnerved, but still curious, he decided to leave the atrium. He'd return to the Vogel tomorrow. And in the meantime, he'd find something from the gift shop to bring to Malia. Whether or not he was placating her–or needed to placate her–he'd never know.

THE gift shop was surprisingly difficult to locate. After walking through the blank-walled gallery, noting that its floor was even wetter than it had been, he returned to the lobby. Expecting the gift shop to be sufficiently prominent, near the entrance, to allure exiting tourists. Or, what had been exiting tourists. But the Museum shop's main doorway was nowhere to be found. Nor was the porter who ought to have been able to point him in the proper direction. All was silent and empty.

Stymied, Pelleas turned on his heel and explored a side gallery. Though he'd visited the Vogel many times before, at least when it had still contained art, he'd never had reason to locate the gift shop. Surely it must be near the front of the building? And yet, apparently, it wasn't.

As he wandered further and further back, gazing up at the bare walls, his irritation with Malia grew. He should never have made her the half-joking promise of a gift. But he knew that now that he had, she *would* be sullen if he didn't present her with some token object. Her attitude toward gifts was the only neurosis he'd ever detected in her. Something about being a billionaire's daughter, he imagined.

Turning into a narrow corridor he hadn't remembered from previous visits, he chided himself for begrudging her the time it would take him to spot a likely offering. It was the least he could do in exchange for all she'd given—

He stopped mid-thought. In front of him was a small, dark, wooden door. An equally small, hand-painted sign to the side of the door. "Gifts." Not what he'd expected. But, dipping his head to avoid hitting the lintel, he entered the cramped space. Nothing about Vogel's architectural monstrosity could surprise him. He thought, as he passed through, that he could just hear the sound of the lobby chiming noon.

Inside, though dimly lit, the shop displayed all of the well-packaged tat that Pelleas had expected. Bad prints of the paintings that had disappeared. A stack of anachronistic daily calendars decorated by embossed golden arabesques. A miniature resin model of the Vogel mansion itself that he considered for a few moments before replacing. Umbrellas with canopies displaying art held by more famous museums. Lots of Van Gogh. Decks of cards. Diaries. Mouse Pads.

Frustrated, he made his way to the counter. Where, drawing in his breath a second time, echoing his reaction to the sight in the atrium, he saw the gemstone. Again. Unembellished. Sitting alone in a small wicker basket with a "sale" sign hand-written over it.

Cautious for reasons that he couldn't analyze, he lifted the red globe in his hand. Heavy and cool to the touch. Obviously a fake, but such a remarkable fake. He raised it up to the low light. And smiled.

He'd present Malia with the stone. And then, when the time came, he'd hope that she left it behind in his studio, as she had with every other gift he'd ever given her. In practice, he couldn't let her take it from him. So, things might become awkward. But he'd worry about that later. For now—

"You're fortunate. That's the last of the bunch."

Pelleas flinched at the voice. Then, feeling foolish for his agitation, he addressed the man behind the counter. He'd not noticed him earlier.

"Thanks," he replied. "Good to know."

The man perplexed him. Not only had he apparently crept up from some hiding place under the register, but he was, like the other men Pelleas had encountered that day, small and elfin with a pronounced hump on his right shoulder. A touch manic.

For a moment, Pelleas believed he was the figure Malia had spotted in the gallery. But then he remembered that the man they'd met before was stooping from the left shoulder. Not the right. And Pelleas, an artist, rarely mistook that sort of detail. Perhaps the two wizened figures were related to one another? Afflicted by the same mirror-image genetic quirk? And took turns manning the gift shop..?

"How much is it?" Pelleas was extracting his wallet from his pocket.

"For you? Nothing."

"What?"

"It's on sale."

Pelleas gazed, suspicious, across the counter. Imagining claxons joining the chimes as he left the building, having shoplifted the gemstone. By now the Vogel's trustees must have installed at least a few security measures. "Nothing?"

"Nothing."

"I want a receipt."

The man giggled. "As you wish."

Performing a complicated maneuver on his register, he ran a slip of paper beneath an antiquated printer, ripped it from the spool, and handed it to Pelleas. Then he dropped the gemstone into a Vogel Museum shopping bag and pushed it across the counter.

Pelleas examined the receipt, stuffed it into his pocket, and accepted the bag. "Thank you."

"You're very welcome, sir."

With ill grace, he left the shop and, after only a few wrong turnings, the Museum.

THE sun was still up when Pelleas reached his studio, and he used the natural light to aid him in finding an appropriate spot to display the red gemstone. For Malia. Kicking aside the Styrofoam otter as he entered, he prowled the space, raising the blinds covering the industrial windows, and opening the skylights.

Eventually, he placed the stone on a stool positioned at the center of the room beneath the largest skylight. Then, retreating several feet from it, he occupied a second stool and gazed at it. He wanted to paint it. Even though he didn't paint. But he did, of course, own paints and canvases.

Feeling a surge of energy he hadn't experienced since Cake Walk, he jumped up from the stool and rummaged about in his materials until he unearthed three or four large canvases, a set of watercolors, and a collection of oils. After a few seconds of hesitation, he set aside the watercolors. The red stone wanted something thick and bold.

Then, though the light was dimming, he began to set up his space. Buzzing and vigorous. He'd commence tomorrow morning. Tomorrow, he'd—

He was startled out of his planning by an insistent droning sound. On. Off. On. Off. And then, interminably, on.

His door. Malia, undoubtedly, wanting to eat another bowl of fish in orange stuff. He briefly considered ignoring the summons. But then he accepted that he'd only pay for the neglect later. Muttering expletives, he shuffled to the door and rolled it open.

It wasn't Malia. Though it was, like Malia, a young woman. Lithe, energetic, and strong. Unlike Malia, however, at least ordinarily, she was also barefoot. Not to mention drenched. And blind. She was observing him—or seeming to observe him—through empty, badly scarred eye-sockets. Otherwise, she was beautiful.

He caught himself. The missing eyes were also beautiful. One thing didn't mar the other. He peered behind her to determine whether she was being helped by a guide. Or even an animal. But the darkening alley outside his loft was empty. Silent.

"Can I help you?" he finally managed.

"I'm wet." She had a faint accent. French or Spanish. Perhaps Caribbean.

"Uh—yes." Pelleas was at a loss. "You are. I've got a towel inside, if that would help."

She stepped through the door. "Yes."

He rolled the door shut and looked about the room. Then, hurriedly, he pulled a folding chair in her direction. "Sit for a moment, all right? I've got a chair here. I'll bring you the towel."

She shook her head and began moving in the direction of the toilet and shower that were separated from the remainder of the space by a long plastic curtain on grommets. She had little difficulty in navigating the area, despite her missing eyes.

"I'll wash in here," she told him. "Then the towel."

She hardly needed more washing, but Pelleas didn't want to argue. "Yes," he agreed again. "Fine. I'll wait out here, then."

She turned her scarred sockets on him. "Don't watch."

He stared at her. Though obviously she couldn't see his reaction.

"Of course not." He cleared his throat. "As I said, I'll be over here. I'll leave the towel"—retrieving a clean one from a free-standing cupboard and handing it to her—"here."

"Good." She disappeared behind the curtain, and he heard the water running.

As she showered, he rubbed his fingertips against his temples and paced the room. He was worried less about his lost time–about the delay in his work on the gemstone–than he was about explaining this development to Malia. She wouldn't be jealous–she was never jealous. But neither would she be pleased. Malia curated her friends with great care, and a blind, barefoot waif with likely mental problems was not her type. She would not welcome the woman into their–her–circle.

Pelleas, however, found himself curious about how the woman had turned up on his doorstep and–sheepishly–what she looked like at the moment, now, behind the shower curtain. No doubt because she'd inserted the image into his mind. Deliberately? He killed the thought. Unkind. And possibly criminal.

Rather, he allowed himself in a pleasurable, dreamlike sort of way to muddle up his impressions of the gemstone with his impressions of the woman. As the water ran, he found himself wanting to paint both of them. Failing to notice as a trickle of damp, perhaps from a clogged drain, pooled beyond the border of his makeshift toilet and began spreading across the floor.

When the woman emerged from the shower–a good hour later–she was wearing the towel he'd provided her, and yet she remained drenched. The towel itself sodden and heavy. But she seemed not to mind. Instead, making her way unerringly to the stool on which he'd settled the red stone, she lifted it, sat, and cradled the stone in her lap.

"Now paint me," she said.

"I–I don't paint," he replied awkwardly. "And I don't do figures."

"Paint me."

He chewed his chapped lips. "The light's gone."

"Paint me."

Pelleas, still habituated to obedience, positioned himself behind an easel, prepared a canvas, and began. Shoving aside all worries about Malia. Forgetting Malia altogether.

AS it happened, Malia never returned. And Pelleas, concentrating on his work, painting night and day with only brief, black periods of unconsciousness to sustain him, failed to notice. Just as he failed to notice the saturation of his loft, the persistently damp state of his clothing and his hair.

At one point, perhaps ten days after the blind woman had appeared at his door, Malia's friend Jen telephoned him, asking whether Malia was with him or whether he'd seen her. And when he'd merely grunted noncommittally, Jen had begun to cry. And then to babble.

Apparently, Malia had become unhealthily fixated on her feet, or her footprints–Jen didn't know, it had all seemed like a joke at the time–

until, without warning, she'd disappeared. No trace of her anywhere. No one knew what had happened—

Pelleas had listened to Jen's monologue for thirty or forty seconds before turning off his phone and tossing it into a puddle. Cake Walk had been two years ago. He no longer cared about footprints. Or feet.

Besides, Jen knew perfectly well that Malia was a self-sufficient person. She could more than take care of herself. Unlike his fragile, fractured muse. He was pleased that the latter couldn't see the art that she inspired. That the gaze went only one way. That, unlike Malia, she controlled nothing.

In fact, the only complaint that Pelleas had about the woman was that she insisted on breaking off their sittings at least two or three times every day to shower. He was more than understanding of compulsive behavior, and so he made no attempt to stop her or, inanely, to cure her. But he did resent the interruptions to his work. Every time it happened. Not to mention that he was having more and more difficulty as the days passed not looking in on her under the water.

Which was a bizarre desire on his part, because it wasn't as though he hadn't seen her nude. On the contrary, he'd painted her from every conceivable angle in every possible position. And he wasn't even attracted to her as more than an art object. She was surprisingly absent erotic pull. But nonetheless, ever since that first night, when she'd laid down the prohibition, the desire to spy on her in the shower had grown.

Until, inevitably, it conquered him. Perhaps three weeks after the woman's arrival, Pelleas gave in to his need. Notwithstanding that he owed her everything. Despite the fact that, because of her, he'd recently sold three of his paintings for more than he'd earned in the previous five years. Having allowed his agent, bewildered but used to artists, to squelch across the boggy floor, umbrella raised against the drizzle that unaccountably fell from the ceiling, and examine the new work. He simply couldn't help it. Pelleas had to see her in the water.

And so, on a warm spring evening, as the sun was setting, he gave in to his craving and crept across the studio. The sound of the shower pattering against the concrete—or, more accurately, pattering against the three or four inches of standing water that now covered the concrete—muffling his approach. Preventing detection.

He felt absurd nearing the shower with such circumspection. She wouldn't *see* him, even if he stood three feet away, with the curtain thrown wide open. But still, he remained stealthy. For reasons he couldn't analyze.

Moreover, once he was in position, he held his breath for eight or nine seconds, preparing. Steeling himself. Finding the proper mental state. Before, tense, he cracked the curtain a tiny inch, put one eye up to the opening, and looked. And fainted. Unable to process the scene.

WHEN he came to, his agent was standing over him. Three days had passed and, worried about Pelleas's silence, he—the agent—had used his own key to enter the loft. Pelleas himself, though damp, was unhurt. The water in which he'd lain unconscious had been warm—May that year pleasantly temperate—and though his skin was loosely wrinkled, he'd sustained no internal damage.

His work, however, was beyond salvage. The paints, the canvases, the sculptures, even the Styrofoam otter—though it was difficult, physically, to know how—had liquified. Melted. They were nothing more than a colorful puddle. Wasted away. And, of course, the gemstone was gone.

Pelleas's agent encouraged him to use the catastrophe as an impetus to greater creativity—to find fertility in the melt. But Pelleas was never able to recapture what the blind woman had brought to him, and eventually his agent had given up. Pelleas's artistic instinct had liquified and drained away along with his work.

And so, Pelleas spent the remainder of his career painting watercolors of fish. The wrong fish. Unable, ever, to capture on the cheap paper he now used the one fish that, as long as he lived, he'd never expunge from his mind. As much as he labored, night and day, to do so. As much as he prayed, daily, to forget. The liquid thing was always there, distracting and blinding him.

He never heard from Malia (or Jen) again.

Dusk

IT was the fifteenth of June when Charlene realized that she didn't know how long she'd been patronizing the car wash. Strange that she was unable to pinpoint the date she'd first noticed it from the freeway off-ramp. Slowed and maneuvered her vehicle onto the premises. She used it now every evening, regarding it as a sort of symbolic gateway between her work life and her dissatisfying personal time in the minutely regulated, sterile residential community in which she lived. "Lived."

Charlene had rented space in the community upon being offered the position of senior site manager for the viaduct project. Daily, she fled the plastic high-rise in her thirty-year-old Ford Bronco to oversee the dismantling of the aboveground expressway that had, for close to a century, isolated the upper reaches of the city. If the project went according to plan—which they never did—she'd likewise be managing, seven months from now, the sinking of the road into a tunnel beneath the old neighborhood. And, depending upon her mood, possibly the renovation in the coming year of the uptown dockside into a space inhabitable by people who preferred not to live in the company of rats, swill, and decay. In the company of visible rats, swill, and decay, that is. Charlene was nothing if not a realist.

But she doubted that she'd be taking on the last of the three assignments. Though the viaduct project represented a milestone in her career–and site manager a position that she couldn't refuse–she disliked the city itself. Its pretensions to gentility–tainting even its grittiest neighborhoods and its most debased, contemptible streets–rubbed her up the wrong way, having been raised, as she had, in a smaller and more properly abject splotch of urban blight a few hundred miles to the north.

She'd taken the antiseptic rooms in the brutally respectable building off the freeway in large part to prevent herself from becoming too comfortable. To remind herself to leave before she found herself trapped. To prompt her to return home when the time came.

The car wash had appealed to her because it had reminded her of home. Run down, scarcely visible from the road, and unfriendly, it was the opposite of welcoming or–more common in the city–didactic. It sneered at passing vehicles, daring them to enter, and radiated an atmosphere of utter indifference as to whether a) the drivers of those vehicles had been satisfied by the services it provided, or b) they were having a nice day.

As far as Charlene was concerned, all businesses ought to operate in such an ambiance–though she knew that her preferences placed her in the minority. Thus, she couldn't very well resist it when she saw the structure glowering up at her from beneath the off-ramp. And she couldn't resist returning to it once she'd been through and concluded that its touchiness was genuine.

Also, of course, she needed the ongoing services of a car wash. Though she parked her truck well away from the active sections of the building site, the Bronco's windows and exposed surfaces were coated with newly accumulated filth every afternoon by the time she closed construction. She could, perhaps, have skipped a day or two between visits to save the finish, such as it was. But having discovered the business–no name as far as she could tell, just a faded red and blue sign above the entrance that read "CAR WASH"–she enjoyed turning her time there into a daily ritual.

Idling in neutral as the multicolored streams of soap and rotating brushes did their work. She felt more at home there than she ever had in her rented rooms with their trite view of the river. And so, gradually, her evening visits had become addictive, a necessary comfort in the midst of the aggravating year-long sentence in the precious city to which she'd condemned herself.

But still, she was bothered on the fifteenth of June by the fact that she couldn't remember when she'd first noticed the place. It seemed now as though she'd always known of it. Always haunted it. Her experiences driving through it unvaried and immutable. Eternal.

Without fail, for example, she entered the establishment fifteen or twenty minutes before nightfall. And without fail, she exited to the west just as the sun was sinking below the horizon. After which, driving a mile or two along surface roads in the gathering darkness, she reached her building's garage, festooned with its collection of notices of new rules and regulations, in pitch blackness. In preparation for another night of rest in her soulless residence.

She slowed and turned onto the ramp leading to the wash tunnel. It was odd, when she thought about it, that the light had never changed. After all, she routinely left her building site at 5:00 in the afternoon. And she'd been doing so for more than four months now, over ever lengthening days. And yet, she always reached the car wash at sunset. Surely, at some point, she ought to have begun entering and exiting in full daylight? Absentmindedly, she swiped her card across the reader–she'd purchased the unlimited wash option weeks ago. Then she decided that she was overthinking the situation, and she relaxed as she maneuvered onto the rails.

THE next evening, on the sixteenth of June, Charlene found herself dwelling on the same anomaly. As she slowed toward the wash tunnel, she repeated to herself that the light didn't make sense. In fact, it was completely inexplicable. But then, she rationalized, the business generally was unusual. Off-kilter. Apparently it even had a reputation among the permanent residents of the city.

Though she avoided as much as possible discussing her personal life with her crews—not that visits to a car wash constituted a personal life for most people (she accepted her limitations)—a few of her more trusted local subcontractors had still warned her away from the establishment when she'd mentioned it to them. When pressed as to why, however, they'd gone silent. Shamefaced. All they would tell her was that the business was said to be owned by a collection of women who had once, so the rumor went, been members of a 1990s-era Riot Grrrl band. Aging now, they still packed the occasional punch.

A curious story, yes, but Charlene couldn't understand what it had to do with the air of disreputability that clung to the business. If anything, especially in this city, the Riot Grrrl connection ought to have granted the place an edge in the market. She herself admired the proprietors in a vague sort of way, if the story was true, for putting away their guitars and investing in automotive detailing when their movement had been coopted by the emergent media conglomerates of the early 2000s. Or something. It wasn't her generation. But whatever the case, the rumors of a Riot Grrrl past on the part of its owners certainly didn't explain the stationing of the sun every time she drove through it. An investigative dead end.

Charlene peered through the streaks of soap at the waiting area just visible beyond the edge of the tunnel. One of the perks of this particular business was the option, should a patron desire, to exit one's car and wait while a worker maneuvered the vehicle through the tunnel on the patron's behalf. And many customers took advantage of the offer because the shape of the tunnel was awkward. Vexing.

Though the wash itself ran straight, pulling a car along rails for a little over 100 feet, the access to the rails was at a near right angle. In practice, this meant that an inexperienced driver was more likely than not to scrape a fender along the outer ridge of the mechanism before properly aligning her car. Charlene had done so a few times before she'd gotten the knack of the space. It was a complicated operation, demanding patience that most drivers, returning from work, didn't have.

And indeed, she noticed that several of the patrons who visited the car wash in the later hours of the day, as she herself did, chose to leave their vehicles to the professionals. Once their cars were through, they retrieved them at the far end of the tunnel. Though Charlene had never actually seen anyone doing that.

Wiping her hand against her window, she tried to summon up a better view of the windows framing the waiting area. Workers had brought two cars through the tunnel ahead of her, and yet

Charlene couldn't see anyone beyond the glass. A situation, like the light, that had now, imperceptibly, begun to bother her.

But then, leaning back in her seat and enjoying the last thirty seconds of the rinse, she dismissed the question. This was her time of peace. She wasn't going to ruin it. To waste it. She tapped the bottom of the wheel with her fingertips as fans blew hot air against the windscreen of the Bronco, pushing beads of water up and over the glass. Squinted as she eased the truck into the sunset. And then half smiled.

The final step in the wash was to wait while three young women—standing at the end of the tunnel beneath a "tips not accepted" banner—toweled off the car. Though Charlene was too inhibited to make eye-contact with the women, and though she was by no means the type to romanticize manual labor, she liked them intuitively. Something about their hats, she'd decided weeks ago, which reminded her of those worn by women in a drawing she'd once coveted on the wall of a wealthy client—"Washer Women of Vannes, Brittany," he'd told her. An image both dour and calming. Much like the car wash. Much like Charlene herself.

The women with the towels weren't charming. Nor did they attempt to communicate beyond stepping back when the drying was complete. But their quiet industry, soaking up the liquid and then squeezing it out into waiting buckets—twisting it from the towels into reddish, whitish, or yellowish pools, depending upon the wax used in the tunnel–was skilled and competent. Their work soothed Charlene. She could have idled, watching them, for hours. Until darkness fell–if darkness ever did arrive here. A thought that jolted her back into a state of mild apprehension. Verging on irritation.

As though sensing her dissatisfaction with her visit this evening, the women toweling off the Bronco worked more quickly than they ordinarily did. And when they squeezed the excess water into the waiting buckets, it was distinctly red. Not pink. Not tinted. But red. Thick, even.

Moreover, as Charlene squinted in the direction of the spare buckets, she was certain that she saw one of the women squeeze something solid out of her towel. Something that landed with a splash into the bucket. Something that couldn't have come from her Bronco. It resembled, if anything, a small, shriveled hand.

Rubbing her eyes, she stared more pointedly at the buckets. But the sun was low, the light glaring, and she could make out little beyond silhouettes. Besides, the car behind her was edging out of the tunnel, and she was blocking its way. Chastising herself for her suggestibility–though for what and from whom, she wasn't certain–she maneuvered her truck onto the surface roads. The sky was already turning black.

AT work the next day, Charlene was preoccupied and distracted. Unlike herself. And after snapping at one of her crews—and then apologizing for it (a bigger blunder than losing her temper to begin with)—she shut herself up in her trailer to keep from making serious mistakes. She couldn't wreck this opportunity. Nor did she particularly want, in the abstract, the viaduct to come crashing unchecked to the ground on her watch. Certainly not if the reason was that she was dwelling excessively on the off-putting customer service at her local car wash. The red liquid. The hand.

And yet, she couldn't stop herself from dwelling on it. To the extent that when the machines stopped for lunch, her favorite subcontractor appeared at her door to try to jolly her out of her mood by presenting her with a bar of chocolate from that company that had imploded a few months ago. But she didn't like chili peppers in her confectionery, and she wasn't in the mood to be placated. Still, she allowed him to stay, thinking she might learn something from him. He'd lived his whole life in the city. As had six, ten, countless generations of his family. And so, she asked.

He stared at her from under his brows for a few seconds before answering. And then, shaking his head, he spoke. "Just stay away from the place, Char. Take your business elsewhere. Lots of other car washes in the city."

"But *why*?" She knew she sounded petulant, but she needed a specific reason. She was a grounded, practical person. Innuendo did nothing for her.

"Because bad shit happens there." He leaned back in his chair and popped a piece of the chocolate she hadn't eaten into his mouth.

" *What* bad shit? That's what I'm trying to find out."

"Bad. Shit." He held her eyes again, level. "Look at you. You haven't been normal since you found the place. Bad shit."

"I can't even remember when I found the place," she muttered, half to herself.

"See what I mean?" He stood to go.

"Wait," she said. "Is there some, you know, story about it? Is it haunted? Built on an old graveyard or a serial killer's dumping ground or something? Anything?"

"Nope." He shrugged. "Nothing."

"What was there before?"

"It's always been there. Nothing was there before." And he left before she could press him further.

She stared down at the linoleum tabletop that took up much of the center of the trailer. Then, coming to a decision, she tossed the remainder of the chocolate bar into a wastepaper basket. She'd take a half-day. Claim illness. They'd believe it after her behavior this morning. And she'd reach the car wash in the middle of the afternoon—before the sun was anywhere near the horizon. Surprise them. Break the spell.

And yet, following a fifteen-minute drive across town in sparse, midday traffic, the light, familiarly, began to change as she slowed along the off-ramp and turned toward the entrance of the establishment. Looking up as she moved to swipe her card, she saw that the sun was hovering just above the "CAR WASH" sign, as it always did, infusing the air with its habitual reddish tint.

Unwilling to be daunted, she pressed ahead anyway, before idling in neutral behind the three vehicles queued up in front of her. This time, she took care to note the people who exited their cars for the waiting room: an elderly man in an unnecessarily belted and buttoned brownish trench coat who had been driving some sort of Honda, and a woman managing a toddler as she stepped down from a large Lincoln SUV. A purple plush elephant clipped to the strap of her handbag to distract the child as she paid and walked through the swinging door.

Workers wearing the establishment's customary headgear took control of the vehicles that had been left and maneuvered them onto the rails. The car directly in front of her—a red Mazda coupe—had retained its original driver. Though it had also, despite much careful inching back and forth, scraped against the mechanism as it turned onto the rails. Charlene could hear the screeching.

She, too (unusually), brushed her fender as she moved into position, concentrating as she was on the customers who had entered the waiting room. But the scratch was minimal—and she'd never repaired the Bronco's scars, along the same stretch of paint, from her first few encounters with the business. She was less worried about the damage to her truck than she was about losing sight of the woman with the child and the elderly man in the trench coat.

As the first jets of water hit the sides of the Bronco, she kept the three figures in view through the waiting room windows. The man was reading a magazine, looking pained. The woman was holding the toddler, bouncing about the room, trying unsuccessfully to calm what looked like an incipient tantrum.

Charlene lost sight of them when the brushes came down, rolling up and over the truck's bodywork. But thirty seconds later, she could see the windows again, and all three were still present. The man glaring, irritated, down at his magazine, and the woman looking embarrassed as she shushed the wailing child. A heavy stream of water—the last rinse—descended, and the waiting room disappeared again. As the hot air blew the water away from the glass, however, Charlene could see the waiting room a final time. It was empty now. No one behind the windows. No one anywhere.

She gripped the wheel as the mechanism dragged her Bronco through the last few feet of the tunnel. Willing the Mazda in front of her to move itself out of the way so that she could see the other end of the ramp. They must have collected their vehicles and gone. No need to wait. Charlene was letting her mind run wild after her conversation with the subcontractor.

But when the Mazda had finally gone its way, and Charlene had positioned her truck under the "no tips accepted" banner, the area was empty. All she could see was the sun was sinking below the horizon. The last light from the west blinding in its intensity. Shading her eyes with her hand, she glanced down at the clock embedded in the dash. 8:20 pm. More than nine hours had passed since she'd left the building site.

As the women with the towels approached her vehicle, she forced herself to keep from shaking. This issue—problem—whatever it was—had nothing to do with the car wash. She was having some sort of breakdown. And, as her subcontractor had hinted, she'd need to fix it—quickly—in order not to lose her position. Possibly her career.

She stared straight ahead as the women dried the truck. She didn't want to see them. She didn't want to think about them. But, try as she might, she couldn't resist peeking at them one last time as they wrung out their towels over the waiting buckets. Red water again. Thick and bright. Far more copious than made any sense.

And surely the clumps of greying hair that they were wringing into the buckets couldn't have collected in the interstices of her truck? Or the knotted belt of a faded brownish trench coat? The sodden purple elephant with the clip, and the three fingers of the hand of a tired woman, one still wearing a wedding ring–

With a squeaking sound she hadn't realized she was capable of making, Charlene floored the accelerator and skidded away from the women with the towels. Onto the nearest surface street. She hoped that she hadn't hurt any of them as she'd fled. But she also didn't care all that much one way or the other. The solution to her problem was simple: find another place to wash the truck. Or leave it dirty. The business was messing with her mind.

WHEN Charlene woke the next morning, she was distressed to find sunlight streaming in through the bedroom window. She'd overslept. Which never happened. Perplexed, she sat up and pushed the eiderdown off her legs. Deciding, as she found clothing to wear, that she disliked her rented rooms as much in the daylight as she did at night. And then she checked the alarm clock, baffled as to why it hadn't woken her.

4:45 AM. Fifteen minutes until it was set to ring. She looked out the window again. Bright sunlight. Annoying, healthy people sculling on the river. Returned to her alarm clock. 4:46 AM. Refusing to be browbeaten, she pulled on her clothing with slow deliberation. Then she walked out to the plastic kitchenette and investigated the clock on the microwave.

4:51 AM. Removed her phone from its charger. 4:51 AM. Opened the likewise plastic blinds shading the large window at the edge of the living area. A stunning beam of light reflected off the roof of the atrium attached to the museum with no art struck her, almost painfully, in the eye. After which, a few diseased pigeons fluttered about, evoking plague.

She shut the blinds, made herself a cup of instant coffee, and grabbed her keys. There was nothing wrong with arriving at the site early. Especially since she'd taken the half-day yesterday. Instead of questioning the sunshine, she'd appreciate the daylight journey. A pleasant drive.

When her crews began to arrive, they were disgruntled to see her already at the base of the viaduct, inspecting their work. But rather than mocking or goading her, as they would have done ordinarily, they meekly went about their business. Subdued. Avoiding eye contact. And Charlene retreated into her trailer, chiding herself for continuing to radiate whatever disquiet was still dogging her. Unable to pinpoint what the problem was. Closing the blinds to block out the insistent sun.

At 10:45, her favorite subcontractor appeared again, bearing a cup of real coffee. He placed it in front of her on the linoleum tabletop, lowered himself into the seat opposite, and unwrapped a bar of chocolate. They were giving it away for free now. She pretended, badly, to be immersed in paperwork.

"Char," he said, "you've got to see someone about this. Before the city gets itself involved, and you wind up blackballed."

She tidied up the stack of papers in front of her. Slid the lot into a branded leatherette briefcase the city had gifted her under better conditions. Her eyes still averted. "I don't even know what's wrong with me. Who do I see?"

"Well," practical, "why are you hiding in here rather than doing your job?"

"The light is bothering me."

"See an eye doctor."

"I'm frightened."

"Of what?"

"I don't know."

"See a shrink."

She laughed. Looked up at him. "I don't do therapy."

He tossed the empty wrapping from the chocolate bar into the wastepaper basket. "Look, Char. You're giving the guys out there the heebie-jeebies. They're not going to put up with it much longer. And you know how many people are waiting in the wings to snatch this job when you fail–"

She stood. "Yes, I know. Thanks."

"No problem."

She took another half-day, avoided the car wash, and returned home. "Home." All she needed was rest. She'd been pushing herself too hard. Fixating on the unimportant. Becoming suggestible.

The windows of her Bronco were so filthy that she could scarcely see through them as she drove, but she pulled over twice to wipe away what she could. And she made it to her building with sufficient visibility through the smeared mud that she avoided colliding with pedestrians or other vehicles. She thought she might have hit a pigeon, but she didn't stop to confirm her suspicion.

When she reached her rooms, she closed all of the blinds to block out the sun, and she double checked to be certain that her clocks were charged and working properly. Then she lay back, tense, on her bed and worked her damnedest to relax. Angry and frustrated that she wasn't at the site, exercising her talents. Doing what she did best.

Eventually, despite her exertions, she slept. Though she wasn't certain as to when or for how many hours. The light trickling in from between the cracks in the blinds never changed. And when she woke the next morning, the sun was still high and emphatic–though her clock told her it was 3:22 in the morning.

Something was wrong. Something more than insufficient rest. And so, bowing to the inevitable, Charlene took advantage of what she'd always thought of as the laughably thorough healthcare coverage the city had contributed to her employment package, and she bullied herself into an appointment with an optometrist. At 11:00 in the morning that day. Under the bright sun.

But her eyes, it transpired, were normal. And she refused to allow the doctor to probe further, questioning her state of mind, once she'd feebly described to him her experiences of the past week. The unchanging light. The need to shut the blinds day and night, to shield her face–

Instead, making use of another of her benefits, she saw a psychologist the following day. An experience that was precisely as useful as Charlene had always believed it would be. When the woman offered her a cup of herbal tea and asked her whether she'd experienced important life changes recently, Charlene politely thanked her and left the room. She knew what her problem was. Of, if not what her problem was, at least where it had originated. She'd simply been avoiding it. Time, now, to face up to it properly.

Thus, the next day–she paid no attention to the hour, she knew when she would arrive–she drove her mud-encrusted Bronco to the car wash. And as she turned into the entrance, the sun began, mercifully, to sink below the "CAR WASH" sign. The light, incrementally, to mellow.

Rather than maneuvering her vehicle onto the rails, however, Charlene opened the driver's side door, stepped out, and waved to the woman overseeing the waiting area. Taking her time because the establishment was quiet, the woman nodded and approached her. Gazed, silent and serious, at Charlene once they were close enough to communicate.

Indicating the open door, Charlene stepped away from the Bronco. "Key is in the ignition."

Then she turned her back on the woman and walked into the waiting area.

It was a dreary spot. Through a line of windows facing forward, she could watch the cars passing and the brushes at work. And through a narrow gap in the west wall, she could see the sun sinking. Aside from the windows, the room was decorated by two rows of mustard-colored plastic seats bolted to the floor at either end of the space, gaps in the armrests where ashtrays had once been embedded. The door handle was faintly sticky.

Charlene didn't mind. Lowering herself into a seat at the end of the far row, she lifted what she thought was a discarded automotive magazine, but turned out to be a coupon book for a supermarket that had gone out of business six years ago. She set it to the side. Then she watched as her Bronco entered the wash tunnel. The first spray of soap. The brushes.

As the truck passed, she realized that she wasn't as concerned as she had been about the state of her project. The viaduct could take care of itself. It would come down with or without her help. She needn't have worked herself into such a state about it.

She leaned back, awkwardly, in the mustard-colored chair. The last of her Bronco was disappearing into the final rinse. Then she glanced up at the window facing west, watching the sun disappear. A paper daily calendar she hadn't noticed earlier was affixed to the wall just to the side of the window frame. In the quickly diminishing light, she saw that today was the twenty-first of June. The summer solstice.

And then the room went black.

THUNDER

BEN had been shaving his head for three months now, ever since Jerome, the Resident Choreographer of the City Ballet, had offered him the role of the first of the three Graces in the Company's revival of *Mercure*. He winced as he ran a razor over a patch of insistent stubble. It grew back so fast. He hadn't counted on that. But how could he have known? At sixteen, Ben hadn't properly begun shaving his face, much less any other part of his body.

He rubbed a towel over his clean, bald pate. Jerome had also found him papers and identification that rendered Ben officially nineteen. His birthday less than a week away, in fact, on the twenty-eighth of July. A day to celebrate.

And just before that, like some latter day urban Orpheus who knew better than to look back, Jerome had lifted Ben out of the squat in which he–Ben–had spent the previous four years. Depositing him in this airy collection of rooms, with their bay windows and their painted moldings, these rooms, in fact, in which he was now removing his body hair. Disgruntled though he might be by the process.

He tossed the towel into a hamper. The rooms were shared with three of the Lighting Director's flunkies because Jerome wasn't foolish in his generosity. But the four of them split three bedrooms and two bathrooms among them, which was more space and more privacy than Ben could remember enjoying since his dim childhood. And a charming, antique tram trundled like clockwork up and down the center of the boulevard beyond their windows every fifteen and a half minutes. Ben liked watching it pass as he ate his cornflakes in the morning.

Thinking of cornflakes, he wandered barefoot, in his underwear, to the kitchen. It wasn't morning–in fact night was falling–but he still liked his cornflakes. Then he found himself a bowl and a spoon. Rummaged about in the refrigerator and pantry for milk and the cereal box.

Naturally, Ben had assumed when Jerome had approached him at the needle exchange under the disused viaduct that the latter's talk of ballet had obscured some more prosaic motive. Or desire. Or set of desires. And even when Jerome had explained the role to him–dancing around a polystyrene fountain wearing nothing but large false breasts, also polystyrene, women's pointe shoes, and several strings of pearls, the last of which would be teasingly removed so that the lead, Mercury, could steal them–Ben had drawn the obvious conclusions.

Though remarkably specific and, as it turned out, not prosaic at all, the general tone of Jerome's request was not outside the realm of what Ben had provided to other clients. Nor, of course, was he was shocked or insulted by it. Ben was far from fastidious. And the pay was certainly reasonable.

He poured the cornflakes into the bowl, splashed milk onto them, and settled himself in the bay window to watch the tram and the pedestrians. The last of the sunset. It was only when Ben had followed Jerome to the rented sedan with the tinted windows that the situation had become unsettling. Especially given Ben's expectations and previous experiences.

Rather than making the commonplace move once they were both in the car, Jerome had instead avoided touching Ben altogether, sitting as far from him as the leather bench allowed. And ten minutes later, when the driver had stopped outside the building in which he–Ben–was now eating his cornflakes, Jerome had handed him a set of keys, identification, and sufficient cash to stretch the seams of the wallet that contained it. After which, he'd ordered Ben to show himself at the City Theatre at eleven the following morning.

Only the knowledge that his cash would be appropriated the moment he set foot in the squat had prevented Ben from fleeing once he'd alighted onto the pavement and watched the sedan's taillights disappearing in the direction of the Malaysian district. But since he'd nowhere else to sleep that night, and since the building intrigued him, he'd used the keys to unlock the heavy front door. He'd then walked, slow and cautious, up the wide, carpeted, curving steps, examining as he climbed the framed botanical prints that decorated the gold-and-red papered walls.

Ben now knew that the two floors above his rooms were occupied by a reclusive old woman who appeared only between two and three in the afternoon, smelling of gin and wearing a silk dressing gown and a tiara, whereas the three floors beneath him were home to a frighteningly healthy professional couple, their two small girls, their poodle, and a live-in nanny. At the time, however, as Ben had ascended the spiral staircase, he'd been convinced that something violent and potentially fatal awaited him. He'd heard tell of such scenarios before, from friends in the squat, many of whom had already amassed large collections of harrowing stories of narrow escapes from precisely this sort of building, in just this type of neighborhood.

As it was, though, the most alarming development was that one of the lighting flunkies with whom he now shared his space had met him in the hallway, wearing boxer shorts and wielding a tennis racquet. Having heard the floor squeak. When Ben had begun to explain himself, the man had lowered the tennis racquet and waved him into silence. Rubbed his eyes.

"You're Jerome's, right? Last of the Graces? The third bedroom's yours. It's small, but it's private." Scratching his cheek, he'd retreated into the darkness of the hall. "We can talk tomorrow if you want to swap."

Ben had stuffed the wallet into the front of his trousers, found the door to his bedroom, and flipped on the light to discover a pristine, newly-made bed. He'd then lowered himself onto the clean blankets. While keeping his shoes and leaving the light on. Just in case. He wasn't stupid.

And yet, all that Jerome had told him had turned out to be true. When Ben, half-sheepish and half-defiant, had presented himself at the stage door of the City Theatre the next morning—scenting, if nothing else, additional cash—he'd been admitted without demur by a thin, elfin woman with hair dyed so skillfully blue that it looked natural. She'd, in turn, brought him to the stage, where he'd met the remainder of the Company, including the other two Graces.

At which point, Ben had relaxed, no longer alienated and alone. Though they'd tried to hide it beneath a bullet-proof, if effete, disdain, Ben had sensed at once that they shared his background. He could smell it on them. And besides, he was First Grace. They were his bitches. All was right with the world.

He lifted the bowl to drink the last of his milky cornflakes. Since then, the Company had become his home. More comfortable, certainly, than the squat had been. And indeed, the only real complaint he had at this point, three months later, was that Jerome apparently wanted his Graces bald—hairless, in fact—in addition to sporting false breasts and women's pointe shoes. And the depilation was becoming a burden.

"You're going like that?"

Ben rose from his chair, considered his underwear, and then looked up. "You don't think he'll like it?"

"He'll like it too much." Dave, the lead lighting flunky—at least, he thought it was Dave; Ben had difficulty telling them apart—was wearing chinos and blue button down shirt. His nondescript brownish hair was wet and combed back. Ben envied the tech people their sartorial freedoms. No expectations.

"Will he mind if I skip it this time?" Ben rubbed his smooth head. "I'm a little tired."

Dave looked at him without speaking.

"Right." Ben dropped his empty cereal bowl into the sink. "I'll be ready in five minutes."

His other complaint—one he felt churlish entertaining, given his previous life—was Jerome's insistence that the Company, in its entirety, never, *ever* miss a party. And there were so very, very many parties. Too many. Nearly every night now that *Mercure* was set to open in two days. He sighed as he approached his wardrobe to select appropriate clothing. He'd wear something tight.

AS Dave, the other lighting flunky, the third one, and Ben approached Jerome's building, black clouds began to gather to the south of the city. Infusing the air, which had been hot and stifling for days now, with a tangible electric charge.

Ben raised his hand to run it through his hair, remembered that he hadn't any hair, and let it fall back to his side.

Some time ago, Jerome had purchased an entire block of lofts at the edge of the Malaysian district. Partially renovated factory space frequented by artists and artistic hangers-on, it had once been—at least according to the more informed dancers in the Company—the primary studio of that tragic conceptual artist. The one who had burst onto the scene with "Wedding Cake," had proved his staying power and versatility with the pornographic fish paintings, and then, inevitably, had broken down. Last anyone had seen of him, he was boarding a Greyhound bus heading north. Beyond the viaduct. Clutching a child's set of watercolor paints that appeared to be melting.

Ben had never followed that world—focused as he'd been until three months ago on keeping himself fed and free of fatal injury—but he'd cultivated a talent for accommodation in the squat, and he learned quickly. Therefore, when they told him of the building's history, he nodded sagely. Knowingly. The tragic artist. Wedding Cake. Pornographic fish. Right. He wasn't going to argue.

Though he also knew, more practically, that the renovated factory was centrally located for Jerome between the City Theatre, where he himself ruled, and the culinary section of the Malaysian district, where his ex-wife had reigned as uncontested despot for more than a decade. Undaunted by the loud and public dissolution of their marriage. Perhaps inspired by it.

Jerome's ex-wife was an institution, more beloved by the city than even Jerome was. In addition to the more commonplace Southeast Asian fare that she served in her larger, popular restaurants, Jerome's ex-wife also served, in her tiny, exclusive corner café, a geographically non-specific, and possibly not entirely legal, turtle soup, "retribution soup," that was, according to the critics, unmatched. Though the same people in the know who remembered Wedding Cake—or was it Cake Walk? Unimportant, it was years ago—also claimed that the true secret to the soup was the collection of spices that Jerome himself prepared by hand with a mortar and pestle—and continued to prepare, even though he was no longer legally bound to the woman or to her establishment—before tossing it into the cauldron. Addictive soup. If unfortunate for the turtles.

Jerome's ex-wife lived for the most part—when she wasn't sourcing turtles—with Jerome and his current wife in the sprawling collection of lofts that they collectively owned. Happily and, it seemed, profitably. As did several dancers. And a large eel with angry red eyes and a disconcerting intelligence, occupying a tank on the top floor of the structure. Or, at least, that's what those who'd inadvertently stumbled upon the thing, searching for the toilet, claimed. Others said it didn't exist. Jerome's house was a confusing sort of edifice.

One never knew what one might encounter around a corner or curled up inside a drainpipe.

No one ever saw the current wife. Barbara. Very pretty, people said. Reclusive. Responsible for the occasionally forbidding atmosphere surrounding the place. And for those rare occasions when the darkest clouds gathered overhead, when the lightning struck a touch too close for comfort, and when guests, emphatically, weren't welcome.

As Ben, Dave, the other one, and the third arrived that evening, however, the building was open and receptive. No more sinister than it ordinarily was. The steel door was rolled up and secured in place to let the hot, heavy summer air into the public rooms, and the space itself was roiling with bodies in various states of undress.

Upon entering, Ben kicked aside an unwieldy chunk of melted pinkish Styrofoam that somewhat resembled a cat. And then he ducked as an axe, hurled from the other side of the room, embedded itself in the wall where his head had been a few seconds before. Laughing politely.

Jerome was already intoxicated. At a certain hour—or, more accurately, at a certain blood-alcohol level—Jerome invariably began to throw the axe. While encouraging others to do the same. Apparently, it had started early tonight.

Ben wrenched the axe out of the wall and crossed the room to return it to Jerome, who was holding court in a chair placed to the side of a drain with odd staining around it. Paint, perhaps.

The remains of a shower curtain pushed to the side. Sprays of mold spreading across an ever-dampish back wall.

After nodding a greeting to the little man with the hat and the erection–some sort of trustee, he assumed; the man was a fixture at these parties, and no one ever mentioned the erection–Ben presented the axe to Jerome. Ceremonial. Jerome, in his customary bare chest and red and white pyjama bottoms, grinned at him.

"Benjamin!" He accepted the axe and then hurled it back across the room. A low rumble disturbed the clouds outside the window. "Threatening weather. I'm pleased you've come."

"Thank you for inviting me."

"So polite. A good boy." Jerome handed him an hors d'oeuvre on a stick. "Try it. Barbara prepared them."

Ben took the stick and smiled. "She's very talented."

His training in the squat serving him well–little could overtly disgust him–Ben turned to face the crowd. Still holding the meat on the stick. Looking amiable and interested, despite the fact that the meat was, unmistakably, a human ear. He refrained from biting into it.

Instead, he wandered, careless, through the bodies, the sweat and the heat rising, until he knew that he was no longer in line of sight. Then, allowing his stomach finally to heave, he thrust the stick with the ear into the head of the Styrofoam cat. Hoping that somewhere, up north, the tragic conceptual artist would approve.

After that, resentful, he danced with dutiful abandon to the music Jerome was pumping into the room. Little more than bass at this point. Dave, the lighting flunky—not to mention the other two—he was confident, would never have been presented with an ear on a stick. Never have been forced to dance with this precise, exact lack of restraint. They were protected. They could wear chinos. Keep their hair.

Whereas for Ben, the constant parties were obviously some sort of examination. A final test to determine whether he was up to performing *Mercure*. Opening now in *less* than two days, if the off-putting rows of antique clocks affixed to the exposed ducts in the ceiling were accurate. The storm clouds outside growled more emphatically. And Ben slowed his dancing. If he didn't leave soon, he'd be forced to pay for a taxi back to his rooms. And his cash was diminishing. Quietly, he slipped out through the steel door. No one noticed his departure.

THE next night, Jerome permitted the Company a rest from the incessant parties. Doubtless because their opening was tomorrow, the twenty-eighth of July, Ben's newly minted birthday. But the rehearsal that afternoon had been worse than any ten parties. Brutal. Demoralizing.

All of which meant that now, attempting to recover, Ben, Dave, and the other one (the third was sleeping) were sitting, exhausted and reclined across three purplish leather sofas–Jerome's chosen décor–drinking can after can of beer. The room they occupied had been the library when their building had been a single-family home, and embedded bookcases lining two of its walls served as shelving for extraneous lighting equipment, cords, and Dave's tennis racquet.

"He's going to burn the place down," Dave was saying. "I know he is. I can feel it in the air."

The other one nodded, morose. Ben had never heard him speak, which hadn't bothered him in the past. He'd seen worse in the squat. But now, the speechlessness of both the other one and the third was making him feel uncomfortable. Verging on frightened. Their continued silence struck him, on a sudden, as not quite human.

And the final rehearsal, as Dave was hinting, *had* felt more–dangerous–than was strictly necessary. Not only had Jerome insisted that each of the sixty-six spotlights he'd had mounted on stakes across the stage be flooded with twenty percent more voltage than they'd been built to handle, but he'd reconfigured entirely the last forty-five seconds of the Graces' dance. Leaving it close to unrecognizable.

Moreover, when Ben and his compatriots had failed to memorize the new steps immediately, he'd screamed at them that they were his props, his objects, and that they'd damned well better start acting like them. Cowed, all three had tried harder. But the results had been middling. None of the three reacted well to abuse. Their backgrounds.

And even leaving aside the crackling spotlights scattered throughout the scene and the shouting, Jerome's changes were disconcerting. Wrong. Now, for example, rather than running, enraged, after the thief, Mercury, and exiting stage right, Ben and the other two Graces were to be lifted on hooks over the lights and hoisted into the scrims, tossing their fake breasts into the audience along the way. But the timing of the lift was impossible to align with the swooping, saccharine music. And after the third or fourth repetition, the chafing of the harness alone had begun to provoke in Ben an atavistic adrenal response. Though, of course, he'd damped it down. Viciously.

Having experienced this life, he'd silently hectored himself as he'd lobbed the polystyrene breasts in the direction of the empty house for the eighth time, he couldn't lose his position with the Company. Not now. There was nothing left for him. Not even the squat. Not even his identity. His birthday.

He rubbed the sore skin on his head with the palm of his hand. "Can't you guys, you know, siphon off some of the current, or something? Make it safe again?"

Dave fixed him with a withering stare. "'Siphon off some of the current?' Do you even know what that means?"

"No," Ben admitted. And then, in defense of Jerome (and himself): "but he knows what he's doing, right? I thought he was the best in the business."

"You know what happened on the opening night of his last show?" Dave refused to be placated.

"No."

"The theatre burned to the ground."

"Oh."

"Do you know what that piece was called? The one that ended it all? In Houston?"

"No."

"*Overvoltage.*" He snorted. "Experimental, apparently."

"Oh." Ben sat upright on the sofa and rubbed his eyes. "So, if he's such a—a fire hazard—why do they hire him? He's worked in hundreds of cities, all over the world. Hasn't he?" Searching for a crack in Dave's certainty. "Hasn't he?"

"Best in the business, like you said," Dave was quiet for a few seconds. Then he continued. "And the theatres don't always catch fire. Only sometimes. So the patrons and donors run a cost-benefit analysis. Keeping in mind that dancers are always expendable."

"Wait." Ben was frowning across at him. "It's happened more than once? I mean, more often than *Overvoltage*? Not just in Houston?"

"Officially," Dave said, "it's never happened. Not even in Houston. There's always a natural explanation. Gas. Tectonic plates. Freak lightning strike. But unofficially? One in every five. Recently, more like one in every four. Jerome's getting edgy, and the critics love it."

"And the dancers?"

"Are expendable," Dave repeated.

Ben squeezed his eyes shut. Then he opened them again. "How long have you been working with him?"

"Always." Slight shrug.

"How long, 'always?'"

"Always 'always.' Never anywhere else." He paused. "It's a good gig. Jerome's creative. Lots of energy. And I like the parties."

"Always."

"You don't have to show up tomorrow, you know." Dave was looking down at his hands. "Others before you have figured it out and done a runner on the opening. He won't track you down. And if you take off an hour or two before the curtain, he'll be all tied up. You'll have a head start."

"But I like it." A weak response. If honest.

And Ben did like it. He liked everything about the Company. About the dance. All of it. And now that it appeared to be flawed, like the rest of his life, he was feeling a familiar, creeping desolation beginning to knot itself up his chest. A desolation that, in turn, left him willing, after all, to sacrifice himself to Jerome's choreography. To *Mercure*. Why not?

Dave rose to his feet and stretched. "Then don't run away. I get it. He's riveting. And

Mercure's a fun piece." He began walking in the direction of his bedroom. "But take my advice, Ben: when they strap you into that harness tomorrow night, be certain that you can reach the release button on your own. Because no one else is going to help you. That I know."

The other one had fallen asleep on the sofa, a victim of the nine or ten cans of beer he'd imbibed. He was gently snoring, unaware of the drift of the conversation. And so, effectively alone, Ben stood to follow Dave. He'd need his sleep before the opening tomorrow.

JEROME grew larger and larger—metaphorically—as he paced backstage, haranguing his dancers in the five minutes before curtain. Mirroring, or echoing, the luxuriant grey clouds that had hung low over the city for more than a week now. Refusing to break. Denying release. Expanding and sucking in energy and moisture, until the atmosphere was both unbearably dry and unbearably sticky. Whichever one felt, impossible to ignore. One hesitated to strike a match over the radiant concrete, imagining the conflagration that might ensue.

Not that the ominous air had put off the City Ballet's patrons. The house was packed. And a seething line of the less fortunate ticketless stretched away from the box office, reaching at one point the edge of the Malaysian district. Yet still, the clouds descended. Breathing became difficult.

Ben, however, in his pointe shoes, pearls, and breasts, paid no attention to the atmospheric or artistic tension as he stretched in a disused green room. Though he understood Jerome's style—terror rather than encouragement—he also knew that Jerome's presence would do nothing for his own performance. And the Graces didn't appear until the second tableau. He'd have time to center himself, to work through the new choreography in his mind, and—above all—to prepare himself for the harness.

Two minutes before the switch to the second tableau, he stole into the wings to watch the end of the first scene. The women representing the signs of the zodiac were finishing up their celebration of the love Apollo and Venus. Too fast, however. Far too fast. In fact, they appeared to Ben to be paying almost no attention to the music, which, against their jerking, frenetic movements, remained stately. Ironically benign.

So fast were they moving, indeed, that their feet were leaving slide marks all over the stage. Or, no. Ben peered at the discoloration more carefully. Not slide marks. Scorching. Their shoes were sending up small flurries of smoke everywhere they hit the ground. Turning the stage blackish in the process.

He ran his hand over the smooth skin of his head. Friction, he supposed. It wasn't impossible. Though he was glad when the tableau ended. It hadn't looked right. And when he'd glanced across the stage to Jerome, grinning at him from the opposite wing, he'd shuddered.

The Resident Choreographer had grown still larger. His red and white dress shirt billowing out behind and around him like flames. While the growling thunder of the incipient storm beyond the theatre doors sounded as though it were coming from inside the building. From somewhere up in the scrims.

But Ben was a professional–or, at least, so he continued to tell himself, having spent his three months with the Company–and he set his disquiet to the side when the brief overture to the second tableau began. He'd worked hard. He would perform well. Make a name for himself.

Without speaking, he lifted his arms to allow the wardrobe people to secure him into his harness. And then, focused, he leapt out onto the stage. Began his labor.

The boards were still hot from the signs of the zodiac, but they weren't unbearable, and the first minute and a half of the Graces' dance was flawless. Better than it had ever gone before, in fact. As he moved, Ben himself fed off the energy of the audience, growing stronger and braver the more intense their interest in him. Feeling, for the first time in his existence, pure joy.

He was also, however, growing uncomfortably hot. Unbearably hot. Unable to understand, such was his concentration, the change in the air. And indeed, it was only when he saw from the tail of his eye the third Grace, behind him and to the left, scream with dismay, stop, and attempt to wriggle from the harness, that he appreciated what had happened around him on the stage.

The sixty-six spotlights had all, simultaneously, caught fire. Spewing sparks and flame onto the curtains, which had in turn ignited as well. Producing a conflagration that had then quickly spread to the scrims behind him. To the blackening, polystyrene fountain.

After which, inevitably, just as he made what he knew was a weak and futile attempt to hit his release button, Ben and the other two graces were hoisted, with a jerk, into their position fifteen feet above the flaming spotlights. Twisting in space, unable to free themselves. Writhing as the heat and smoke rose.

Even so, as the first of his pointe shoes caught fire, Ben squinted toward the tech booth, wanting to catch the eye of Dave, the other one, or the third. Not, of course, in a plea for help. He'd made his choice. They'd respect that. But perhaps in acknowledgment of the time they'd spent together. The beer they'd shared.

The booth, however, was empty. So too was the audience. A vacant house. Moreover, though the shrieking of the other two Graces hanging behind him was certainly loud—deafening even—the sound of the thunder clouds breaking outside was louder. No longer outside at all, if he was honest with himself. Directly above him. Emphasizing the emptiness of the theatre.

Taking a last deep breath of the blistering air, Ben thus did the only thing he could do. He reached behind his back, unhooked his false breasts, themselves beginning to ignite, and tossed them toward the missing audience. As he'd been instructed to do. Playing his role.

Though, it's true, when his skin began to shrivel–no hair to catch fire–he began to forget Jerome's careful choreography. But Ben was talented. A good dancer. He improvised.

TWO days later, the city's major news outlets were still running stories about *Mercure*. All agreed that the firefighters had been aided inestimably by the miraculous break in the weather–the angry, thunderous cloudburst–that had accompanied the conflagration. How else could the disaster that had eradicated an entire historic building have left a total absence of casualties? Everyone accounted for? No identifiable bodies?

Moreover, the commentators continued, though the loss of the theatre itself was unfortunate, it had after all been an old structure, and sufficient online donations had already been collected (twice what was needed within the first six hours, crowd funding being what it was) to construct a new, state-of-the art multipurpose performance space. Perhaps one with a swimming pool.

Not to mention that the critics had gone wild for what they *had* seen of the ballet. To the extent, indeed, that the city was united, for perhaps the first time in its history, in its insistence that the Company and its Choreographer—no longer Resident—return immediately, or at least once a new building suited to their needs had been constructed. The ballet's patrons were slavering for another success. Another *Mercure*.

But Jerome and his dancers were proving difficult to locate. A few people who claimed to be familiar with them said that they'd seen the troupe heading south. Following the weather. Though, of course, these and the other reports were nothing more than rumors. Hot air.

Sunlight

UNTIL six months ago, the corridor had been silent this time of year. In August, that is. Frederic's favorite season to work on campus. The undergraduates were absent. The graduate students were elsewhere, spending their little grants and stipends, contemplating their little careers. And his colleagues were claiming to be in the field conducting research, but were actually intoxicated on various war-torn beaches. Ignoring the warfare.

No one with pretensions to a career, a research agenda, or a sex life languished in his office on a humid day on the fifteenth of August. But Frederic had no pretensions. No life of any kind. Next month, September, marked his thirty-second year at the University. A career glorious in its obscurity. A career during which Frederic had made no impression whatsoever upon the generations of undergraduates who had slept through his lectures, and during which he had published the requisite two monographs necessary to sustaining his position in the Department—and then stopped.

To Frederic's quiet relief, his monographs had sunk and disappeared decades ago, when remaindered books stayed properly remaindered, rather than lingering on in a murky digital half-life, biding their time, waiting to rise up and devour their authors when intellectual fashions changed. Frederic knew for a fact—he'd checked on it—that his books were buried. He doubted that his enemies could even find them—moldering physical objects, stored in annexes and outbuildings, that they were—much less use them as weapons against him, now that he was aging and vulnerable.

Not that he had enemies, of course. Frederic wasn't the sort. In his thirty-two years at the University, he'd not once contradicted a colleague. Not once made a scene at a conference or a seminar. Not once Spearheaded an Initiative. And the handful of graduate students he'd overseen—"mentored," they called it now, though he doubted those promoting the term were familiar with its, to Frederic, ambivalent provenance (as a rule, he was against the indiscriminate slaughter of house guests)—had been as dreary as he himself was. Writing competent, correct dissertations before being swallowed up by minor, provincial technical colleges. Never to be seen again. There hadn't been very many of them, in any case. Frederic was far from magnetic.

And so, in the midst of his humble professional routine—a routine that he'd quite enjoyed for thirty-two years now—August had been his favorite month. A time to return to campus. When the halls and the squares were empty. Echoing. Devoid of energy.

Well: he'd enjoyed the emptiness properly for twenty-eight years, not for thirty-two. Frederic believed in accuracy. Starting from the day, four years into his employment by the University, on which he'd taken possession of the office once held by his predecessor. And his predecessor's predecessor. And the predecessor before that. All holding the same flaccidly endowed, yet still secure (if only just), Chair of Icelandic Literature. All thriving in the far from transcendent void.

The Chair—Frederic's Chair—was a middling to old one. Instituted at the height of the University's regional influence by one of the city's first industrial tycoons (something in chemicals, people said—emergent plastics), its scope was unusual. For, though the tycoon had been wealthy, exuberant, and gratifyingly generous, he'd also been challenged, unfortunately, in his cartographic knowledge. The speech he'd given upon endowing the position—a speech now immortalized in a tarnished plaque that hung to the right of the Department's administrative offices—had placed Iceland on a territorial border with the Grand Duchy of Baden, sharing with Baden its culture, its cuisine, and its clocks. Especially its clocks. No one at the time had thought to contradict him.

And indeed, Frederic had once, in the early days of his career, as a gesture of respect to the man to whom he owed his livelihood, even written an article on Icelandic timekeeping. But this was of course in the years before mocking the people with the money who supported the University's endeavors had become the norm. The article was among his favorite publications. Though it, too, had been carefully lost a good twenty years ago. Frederic had no interest in academic immortality. Attention frightened him.

Much of the world frightened him, which was why he spent such a great deal of time in his office. Though the tiny room that Frederic and his equally anemic predecessors had, for over a century, occupied was undesirable—the reason, he supposed, that he was suffered to retain it—he adored it because he felt safe within its walls. He reveled in its scent of decades-old pipe smoke, not his own. In its view of the drainpipe three storeys below, where October's autumn leaves collected annually into a fecal-colored sludge. He even liked the acoustics.

And the acoustics were, even by the standards of aging academic buildings, disconcerting. A narrow, tube-like space, the room had been squeezed by the eighteenth-century architects of the building between two ventilation shafts, one of which had since become a lift, and the other of which now housed the unisex toilets. As a result, two hundred fifty years later, from one side came a constant murmur that wasn't quite like liquid, whenever the toilets flushed or the sinks ran. And from the other came every word spoken and every sound made in the office on the other side of the lift, enunciated as distinctly as though the speaker were whispering into his ear. Like some trick Renaissance dome. Perhaps the effect was deliberate. One never knew with eighteenth-century architects.

In any case, it was the office on the other side of the shaft—an office that, unlike his own, was large, bright, and desirable—that had begun causing the trouble six months ago. Frederic didn't mind overhearing the occasional conversation from beyond the shaft, it's true. Any more, he imagined, than the occupants of the desirable office minded hearing his own infrequent mumblings into the telephone. Usually requesting office supplies, unsuccessfully, from the Department Administrators.

Because, in the twenty-eight years that Frederic had occupied the space—twenty-eight years during which he'd witnessed fifteen tenants, none happy and none tenured, on the other side of the shaft arrive and depart—not one had pursued conversations that were anything other than banal and mundane. Even in the final months of their contracts. All had been well aware that, insipid though he was, Frederic could easily hear everything that went on in their space. And he did hold the Chair...

Six months ago, however, things had changed. A new Chair of Icelandic Studies (not "Literature"—that remained Frederic's domain) had been endowed, with enormous largesse, by the billionaire inventor of a video game that involved stacking colorful digital cubes on top of one another. A seminal moment in the history of the field. The sort of moment that might well provoke envy in even the most well-adjusted of its observers.

But it wasn't the institution of the Chair itself that troubled Frederic. Nor was it even the funding or the research budget that went along with it. On the contrary, Frederic, far from resenting the position, was charmed by the notion that whoever took it might serve as an attractant to the growing numbers of incoming graduate students who alarmed him with their increasing interest in his past and, worse, his work, now that things Icelandic had become popular once again. The institution of a second Chair couldn't have been more timely, as far as Frederic was concerned. Envy was not the problem. Envy was as alien to Frederic as charisma was.

And though he'd been mildly bewildered by the Search Committee's choice when his new neighbor across the shaft arrived—a small, fastidious man who persistently wore a very silly hat and appeared (though Frederic certainly didn't examine it too closely) to be afflicted by some lamentable form of priapism—Frederic was far from dismayed by the new presence. He wasn't even all that curious. The last to claim familiarity with recent trends in Area Studies, Frederic deduced that the hat and—well, the rest of it—were what the younger generation wanted in an avant-garde intellectual. The crowds of students thronging the newcomer's door the moment he put out his nametag certainly suggested as much. All to the best. And so, in his bashful and antisocial way, Frederic had done what he could to make his counterpart welcome. The mere existence of the Chair, to repeat, wasn't the problem.

Nor was the nametag, though it was an odd one. K. Pelli Fricot. Frederic assumed French or Appalachian–possibly Finnish–though, once more, such issues were beyond his field. And he rarely retained the names of people he hadn't known for at least twenty-five years anyway.

No. The problem–and it had started from the first hour that Fricot had taken possession of the office–was the noise. Horrible noise. Deafening noise. And noise, worst of all, that Frederic simply couldn't account for by any natural explanation. Certainly not by the excited and swarming writers of dissertations both outside and inside of Fricot's space. Or even by the inappropriate use of office furniture (Frederic had heard a bit of that in the early 1990s, and he'd actually found it lightly entertaining; but she hadn't lasted long before taking a job in Comparative Politics at a women's college in the Netherlands). As far as he could tell, Fricot's furniture retained its intended function. Meaning that the noise had some other, baffling, source.

At first, Frederic had concluded, against all reason, that Fricot was keeping animals in his office. The space was certainly large enough to do so. And the sounds—the snuffling of more than one pig, the clattering of hoofs, the wailing of some mournful canid—could hardly have been anything else. But two further observations, collected over the ensuing days, weakened that conviction.

The first was the absence of a smell. The sheer variety of the animals he heard rutting, squealing, and frequently fighting or colliding with one another ought to have suffused the building with a conspicuous barnyard stench. And yet, there was nothing. The corridors, even weeks after Fricot's arrival, still smelt of nothing more than centuries-old sweat and decades-old, now-illegal cigarette smoke. No hint of animal at all.

Second, and perhaps more conclusive, was the behavior of Fricot's students. Had there been animals in the building, they would doubtless have mentioned something, at the very least among themselves. And, given the acoustics, Frederic would have overheard them. But the students said nothing. Though they praised Fricot vociferously, and though they followed him in droves, hanging on his every utterance, not one ever mentioned a pig. Or an angry arctic fox. Or the clamoring of goats.

But then, the students themselves also behaved abnormally upon entering Fricot's office. And indeed, it was the noise of the students, more than the noise of the animals, that eventually provoked Frederic into action. Belated action, yes, but action nonetheless.

For, throughout the first two months of Fricot's occupancy, Frederic had done nothing. That is, nothing aside from clenching his fists and hunching his shoulders whenever he heard the reactions of the students to Fricot's ministrations. But as their screaming intensified, as the evident agony they were suffering beyond the shaft sharpened, Frederic became ever more anxious and confused. Concerned for himself as much as he was for them.

It was, after all, a nightmarish screaming that he heard. Screaming that he'd never imagined could exist in waking life. The screams of people being burned or flayed alive, being subjected to unspeakable pain and torture—certainly not the screams of dissertation writers, at least in his own protracted, if limited, experience.

All of which meant that, sometime in the middle of March, believer in privacy and letting sleeping dogs lie as he was, Frederic resolved to do something heroic about whatever was happening beyond the lift. He couldn't sit idly by as the little mousy girl with the bitten fingernails and the unravelling winter muffler howled in heart-wrenching terror at whatever Fricot was doing to her. And so, squaring his thin shoulders, Frederic had, that day, stalked to Fricot's office, thrown open the door, and taken action.

As it had turned out, however, no action had been needed. The girl was sitting, placid, in the comfortable chair that Fricot provided his visitors. Fricot himself was translating a manuscript he'd unrolled on the desktop in front of him. All was quiet and respectable. Aside, perhaps, from an excessively bright sunlamp drenching the area with almost blinding yellow-white light. A mood enhancer, Frederic supposed.

Mumbling an apology, Frederic had backed out of the office. Bewildered and ashamed. While Fricot and the girl had watched him, the one with genial good humor, the other with overt hostility. Twisting her fingers through the holes in her muffler.

And back in his own cramped space, Frederic had slumped into his lumpy seat. Noting even as he cogitated that the screaming had started up again. He shouldn't have interfered. Obviously. The mousy girl was fine. But the sound—the sound was soul-destroying.

When he thought about it, in fact—a novelty for Frederic in that he generally thought very little about anything aside from the joy he took in his office—he did believe that at least a handful of Fricot's graduate students had gone missing. It was difficult to keep track of them, there were so many. But Frederic was positive that at least some were unaccounted for. Certainly the daughter of that pharmaceutical family that had built the University's biological sciences complex. Mel. Molly. Something. She'd even made the news for a few days.

He'd tapped a fingertip against his chin for three or four seconds. He couldn't make accusations, of course. Nor would he—such was not his role. But, hearing what he heard beyond the shaft, he felt uncomfortably responsible for whatever Fricot was plotting.

Then, leaning back in the chair, Frederic had smiled to himself. "Plotting" indeed. He'd been spending too much time in the realm of the treacherous *jötunn*. They were affecting his mind. And really, what *had* he heard, when he examined the situation? Animals. Some sort of LP or cassette tape or—or digital sound file—no doubt. And screaming. But, as he'd just established, the screaming was an acoustical trick of the building. Nothing about Fricot. And Frederic had certainly had years to familiarize himself with the building's tricks. He liked the building's tricks.

Moreover, aside from the animals and the screaming, the only anomaly Frederic could add to the list of supposed misconduct was Fricot's constant angry conversations on those rare occasions when his students weren't in evidence, conversations that, of course, Frederic couldn't avoid overhearing. Ranting arguments into the telephone—at least Frederic assumed the telephone; Fricot may have been addressing himself—about some elusive woman's arms. Arms like sunlight. Fricot couldn't wait to possess her. He didn't give a damn about the fucking sword...and so on. Odd, yes. But hardly suspicious. The woman who'd taken the appointment in the Netherlands had been far more explicit in her day.

Thus, that afternoon in March, following his embarrassment beyond the shaft, Frederic had resolved simply to let his otherwise hugely successful neighbor have his eccentricities. Frederic himself would ignore the noise. Fricot, despite his oddities, was a familiar type—not the sort to linger in one position for more than a year a two. And Frederic was confident that, come the spring, Fricot would have fluttered off to a better endowed and more prestigious Chair elsewhere. At which point, Frederic himself would be left in peace once more.

But this resolution, determined though it had been, lasted little more than days. As the screaming, howling, rutting, shouting, and keening increased in intensity minute by minute throughout the last weeks of March, Frederic concluded that he couldn't, after all, wait a year. Certainly not three. And when he ascertained, after a careful reconnaissance of the corridor on an empty weekend (and once, pleased with himself, at midnight), that the noise and—more peculiar—the blinding sun-like light persisted even when Fricot himself was absent, he even became gently frightened. Sufficiently frightened that he determined to attempt another exchange with the man.

It took him nearly two months to gather the nerve to approach Fricot a second time. Trailed as the latter always was by his capering, contentious acolytes. But, on a harmless afternoon in early May, near the end of the semester, he did.

Popping his head out of his own door, he asked whether Fricot might speak with him in his office. And Fricot, with his charming smile, waved the students away and complied.

His presence in Frederic's burrow seemed to saturate the place with light, but Frederic failed to comment. Nor did he allow his eyes to fall on Fricot's still prominent condition. Rather, with a rueful smile, he said, trying and failing not to sound querulous: "you're aware, yes, that the lift shaft between our two offices is a terrible conductor of sound?"

"Terrible it is," Fricot affirmed.

"Yes," repeated Frederic, "terrible. And, well, I spend a great deal of time in my own office—"

"—working yourself to the bone."

"Um, yes." Frederic blinked. "And the thing is, I find it difficult to—to *work* in an atmosphere of excessive noise."

"As do I," Fricot replied. "As do I."

"Do you?" Frederic nodded. "Good. I'm pleased that you understand. So—so I hope you'll also understand when I ask whether it might be possible for you to, well, make a bit less noise yourself. In your office, that is."

Fricot slapped his forehead, just under the silly hat, with his hand. "If only I could, my dear man! If only I could." He paused. "If only we all could. This constant chatter. Sometimes," he was speaking confidentially now, "I feel that the world would be an infinitely more inhabitable place if we all–simply–shut up."

"Right." Frederic was unsure that he'd made his point. "Well, so long as you understand, then."

"I'm delighted that we've had this talk."

"Are you?"

"I am." Fricot raised the hat, grinned at Frederic, and left the room.

It was then that Frederic realized that he had a problem.

For, from that May afternoon onward, the clatter in Fricot's office grew to such a magnitude that Frederic could spend no more than five or six minutes in his own office without needing to escape to the corridor to calm himself. To breathe. To rid himself of the horror.

Moreover, and even worse, against all of his inclinations, Frederic had become, by May, adept at identifying the origins of the sounds and screams that he constantly heard. Associating them with specific moments and figures he half-believed he could see in the corridor or floating, mirage-like, beyond his window. He found himself giving them names. Before waiting, tense, for a repetition.

Today, for example, on the fifteenth of August, as he sat staring down at his view of the drainpipe, he believed that what he was hearing through the shaft was the sound, first, of a dog and a goat being exsanguinated alive before both were hung from the branches of a tree. And, second–he pursed his lips–yes, a young girl being strangled.

He closed his eyes and listened more carefully. Nodded. A dog and a goat. Blood spilling. Asphyxiation. The leaves of a tree.

Frederic stood, rubbed his eyes, and came to a decision. Something must be done. He'd take care of the situation today. Otherwise, he'd go mad.

HE'D take care of the situation tomorrow. It was too late in the day today, and he felt a superstitious horror of entering Fricot's office after night had fallen. Besides, tomorrow was Saturday. No one would be in the Department. And he'd thus be able to come prepared to deal with whatever he discovered on the other side of the door. In the absence of Fricot himself, perhaps the reality of the situation would show itself. Perhaps it wasn't as bad as Frederic believed.

Therefore, rather than approaching his counterpart's door, Frederic decided on a leisurely walk back to the townhouse he'd inhabited for the same twenty-eight years he'd occupied his office. Where he'd gird himself for battle. After purchasing a gift for himself–a chocolate bar or a mousepad decorated by one of those naughty fish paintings–from the University bookstore on the way. Yes. That would help.

As he passed into the air-conditioned bookstore, he cast a worried look, as he always did these days, at the empty coffee cup upended to the side of the doorway. Until two months ago, a vagrant with an infant had crouched in the spot where the cup now twitched in the air that escaped the building. Day in and day out. Through every season. And Frederic had always pitied her in a colorless sort of way. He'd never encountered a person who could look ice-cold and frozen beyond misery even in June.

Feeling benevolent one Thursday afternoon, in fact, Frederic had gone so far as to purchase a small cup of coffee from the stand across the square and offer it to the woman holding the child. The gesture was out of character for Frederic. Not because he was ungenerous, but because expressions of gratitude made him feel queasy, and he tried as much as possible to avoid situations in which they might occur. Comforting the homeless was, as far as he was ordinarily concerned, a minefield best circumvented.

To his relief, however, when he'd approached the woman, she'd simply moved her blank, beautiful eyes in his direction, accepted the cup, and looked away. And her eyes *had* been beautiful. Frederic had been briefly startled by the unalloyed perfection of her face.

To cover his confusion, he'd thus retreated into the bookstore to collect himself before continuing on his way. Blushing at his reaction to the woman's appearance. After which, from his position hovering beside the display of ghost-written autobiographies of charismatic politicians' wives, he'd watched her through the glass. Unable to stop himself.

First, he'd noted, she'd eyed the coffee with confusion. And then, for a good two minutes, with suspicion. But then finally, she'd taken a small sip of the drink. Frederic had assumed that what had happened next was a trick of the light. Holding her hand–the hand not clutching the coffee–in front of her face, her fingers spread, she'd watched with something approaching a smile as her fingers had stretched and thinned. Steaming or evaporating into the ether. A second sip, and her body had become thinly transparent.

At that point, a commotion on the upper floor of the bookstore had drawn Frederic's attention, and he'd looked away. And when he'd returned his gaze to the spot beyond the glass, all that remained of the scene was the empty cup, rocking gently on the concrete. Even the baby was gone.

Moreover, from that day onward, he'd never seen the vagrant again. And, though he knew it was absurd, he always felt obscurely responsible for her disappearance. Guilt-ridden.

Served him right, too, Frederic thought to himself as he exited the bookstore with his paper bag full of discounted matcha-infused chocolate (he'd decided against the mousepad). It was only to be expected after he'd drawn attention to himself by consorting with the woman. His strength, he must never forget, was his inconspicuousness. His invisibility. His complete and total lack of engagement with the world.

Thinking of disengagement with the world brought him back to his current troubles. He squinted up at the sun, which was still bright—too bright—overhead. And then he admitted to himself that his decision to wait yet one more day before investigating Fricot's office was another mode of evasion. He was acting the coward.

And therefore, slowing to a stop in the middle of the square—failing to notice the enraged bicyclists who were forced to swerve around him—Frederic changed his mind. He'd solve the problem this evening. Now. If not, he'd never address it, and he'd be saddled by the screaming lift shaft indefinitely.

Pulling a bar of his chocolate from the bag, unwrapping it, and taking a small bite, he turned on his heel—still cheerily ignorant of the commotion he was causing in the square—and wandered in the direction of his building. If he could simply investigate Fricot's office without interruption, he was confident that he'd discover a rational explanation for the noise. And then, even should it continue, he'd likely not be nearly as bothered by it. It was the mystery, more than anything else, that was the source of his anxiety. Or, so he told himself.

By the time he reached his own office, the sun was sinking, and he'd finished his first chocolate bar. Stuffing the empty wrapping into the bag alongside the three others he'd purchased, he unlocked his door, flipped on the light, and wandered to his desk. The noise from Fricot's office continued unabated. The pigs again, mostly, at this time in the evening. Though he thought he might also hear the screaming of a terrorized horse underneath the snorting. A good time to investigate.

Rather than sitting at his desk to collect himself, Frederic thus tossed his bag of chocolate onto the desktop with what he liked to think of as a devil-may-care attitude and collected the universal Department key that he'd borrowed from the then-Department Administrator thirty years ago and forgotten to return. Cradling the key in the palm of his hand, he retreated to the corridor and carefully locked his own office. Steeling himself for the assault.

After that, he stood for three or four seconds in front of Fricot's closed, blank door. Before, swallowing, he used the key to unlock it and enter the room. To size up his foe. To make his first move.

To his disappointment, the space was as calm and quiet as it had been when he'd interrupted the meeting with the mousy girl. But at the same time, Frederic had only a half second to contend with the setback. For also immediately apparent was that Fricot himself was present. Or, the body of Fricot. Holding court at his desk in the ergonomic chair, his hands secured behind his back with fishing wire, Fricot stared across the room at Frederic, as though faulting him—Frederic—for the pusillanimous late arrival. His eyes vacant. His face a deep purple.

Someone, Frederic gradually allowed himself to comprehend, had immobilized Fricot in the chair before garroting him with the telephone cord. He still wore his hat. And his affliction was, if anything, more pronounced. Though, Frederic believed, the state of Fricot's—of, well, his affliction—was a common comorbid symptom of the procedure...

With a small moan, Frederic leaned back against the closed door, horrified by the callous thought. Something was clearly wrong with him—with Frederic—for allowing the observation to form in his mind. He must help the man. Or, not help him, obviously. But—fix—somehow, the scene. Fricot's colleagues and students couldn't find him this way. They'd be gutted.

Sparing no thought for the state of what was, after all, a crime scene, Frederic went to work. The notion of police or detectives never entered his mind. He wasn't that sort of person. When he stayed home of an evening, he watched nature documentaries rather than police procedurals. Never did it occur to him to leave Fricot in state.

First, therefore, he cast about for some sort of tool to cut the telephone cord from around Fricot's neck, and to slice the fishing wire from his wrists. Having retrieved a longish blade—a letter opener in the shape of a medieval Carolingian sword (Frederic smiled to himself when he saw it, reminiscent as it was of the Lincoln Sword)—from the top of the bookcase, he gingerly advanced on the figure in the chair. He wouldn't, he decided, touch the hat.

Swallowing bile, he slid an index finger between the telephone cord and the blood-encrusted skin of Fricot's neck. And after pulling at the cord for a second or two, he loosened it sufficiently to slip the letter opener into place and saw at the plastic. A tedious task. But the letter opener was remarkably sharp, as it turned out, and it slipped through the cord with no resistance in a matter of seconds. Pleased by his progress, Frederic then unraveled the remainder of the cord and dropped it to the ground. Fricot's purple face lolled sickeningly to one side.

To avoid taking in the spectacle, Frederic turned his attention to the ceiling. And frowned. The room, he'd noted irrelevantly as he'd labored, was uncomfortably bright. The work of the sunlamps, he'd concluded, though now that he looked about him, he couldn't see any actual lamps. Recessed, he supposed, but that didn't explain the light shining down on him from the ceiling, provoking in him a nausea almost worse than the task itself was.

But he set aside the thought as well as the churning of his stomach. Important now was freeing Fricot's hands. Before, he supposed, contacting the Department Chair. Or perhaps the Dean? Well, he'd concern himself with one thing at a time.

Circling the desk so that he was positioned behind Fricot's chair, he knelt and slipped the knife between the swelling, meaty wrists. Once again, the blade moved smoothly, almost of its own accord, and Fricot's arms were free. They, too, flopped down and forward.

Before Frederic could develop a strategy for moving Fricot into a position of some dignity, however, he heard a disquieting noise. A revolting noise, in fact, even without the presence of a garroted dead body slumped in front of him. The noise of devious, gnawing, and skittering rodents.

Frederic hated rodents. And ordinarily he would have kept well away from the disturbance—done his best to ignore it and hope that it took itself elsewhere. But the notion of leaving Fricot's bleeding, abused body to the rat—or, given the sound, several rats—was not one that Frederic could entertain. Either he'd have to deal with the rodent (perhaps, he told himself feebly, it was nothing more than a family of urban voles), or he'd be forced to stay in the room with the corpse, protecting it, until the Department Chair—or, possibly, the Dean—arrived to take command of the situation.

Sitting up with the corpse was out of the question. Frederic couldn't even form the thought fully in his mind. And so, stiffening his resolve, he instead oriented himself toward the sound, which was coming from the only part of the room shrouded in darkness. A single, unlit, black corner. Thrumming so insistently that it was as though the sound itself were creating the shadow.

It was an uncanny effect, but at least, Frederic told himself, he could easily pinpoint the source of the commotion. And perhaps he wouldn't have to look at it too closely. It was, after all, dim.

Swallowing once again, he held up the letter opener and advanced on the darkness. The blade, as before, felt obscurely like it was pulling him forward, but Frederic was comforted by the tugging impression, and so he allowed it to do its work. When he reached the shadow and saw what crouched within it, however, he lost his resolve. Indeed, he lost much of his sense of reality.

Whimpering, he closed his eyes, shook his head like a child, and wished the thing away. He couldn't move. He couldn't contend with it. All he wanted to do was to expunge all knowledge of its existence from his mind. He simply didn't want to know.

But the letter opener, even as Frederic wilted to the ground, remained stalwart. Pulling his hand toward the thing in the corner with a force that kept Frederic, if only just, on the proper side of consciousness, the blade sliced into the thing's stinking, fetid skin, twisted itself twice, and withdrew. And Frederic, his task complete, fainted.

HE came to himself a few minutes later in a darkened room, gagging on the smell of blood. Gagging also on what he prayed were the dregs of a nightmare rather than a memory of some actual event that he only half recalled. Whatever was causing his stomach to heave itself into his throat, however, his instinct was to get himself out of the room as quickly as possible. It didn't matter what the source of the smell and the memory might be. He didn't want to think about it.

Still whimpering, he rose to his hands and knees, crawled in the direction of the door—he could just make out the dim glow from the corridor at its edges—dragged himself upright, and, with a trembling index finger, pushed up the light switch. Which operated as usual. Normal, flickering office light—not the blinding sunlamp.

But even in the comforting light, the office had changed. And not in a way to allay Frederic's fears. Fricot, for example, was still sitting behind his desk in the ergonomic chair. He was also, however, grinning at Frederic. Chuckling, if politely, under his breath. Healthy and unscathed. The telephone was where it ought to have been.

Whereas, to the side of the room, lacerated and wheezing in a pool of blood, was the mousy girl. She appeared to be trying to crawl toward him—Frederic—but she was too badly injured to make much progress. After three or four seconds, she gave up on her struggle and, with a final, gurgling rattle, cast an angry look in Frederic's direction and expired.

Frederic himself, having managed unsteadily to rise to his feet, looked down at his hands. They still held the letter opener, and they (and it) were drenched with the girl's blood. As was his clothing. He believed he could also feel it in his hair. With a dog-like yelp, he dropped the letter opener to his feet, where it clattered into immobility.

"Satisfied?" Fricot hadn't changed position.

Frederic shook his head. He couldn't summon up words or a voice to express himself.

"You were curious," Fricot explained. "Now you know."

Frederic continued shaking his head. He knew nothing. Fricot stood and straightened his hat. His erection was as pronounced as it ever was.

"Someone's always got to end it," he eventually clarified. "Otherwise, August lingers. This time, the honor was yours."

Frederic rubbed his forehead with the palm of his hand, smearing blood further across his face.

"What will I do?" His voice was a croak.

Fricot wrinkled his brow, considering.

"You might take up a new research project," he said after a few seconds. "Apply for a grant? The future is bright, my dear old man. The future is bright, indeed."

And with that, he squeezed past Frederic and left the office. Shutting the door quietly, with a click, behind him.

While the body of the girl bled and stiffened a few feet to the left of his desk.

Rain

BRENDAN wasn't eating. Again. Lynn watched him from the other end of the dining table as he mounded the salad into a small hillock at the edge of his plate. Speared a miniscule shred of halibut with his fork, lifted it, and then let it fall surreptitiously to the floor. Not all that surreptitiously, actually. He wasn't troubling to hide his behavior from her.

Sullen, he looked up at her from under his brows, daring her to comment. And silent, she consumed a large piece of the fish, allowing herself to enjoy it. Chef had done well this evening.

Lynn had become used to Brendan's periods of eating difficulties–she didn't call them, collectively, a disorder because they rarely lasted more than days or weeks at a time–in the four years he'd lived with her. They were always worse in the autumn. When the drizzle spat against the tall windows to their left, as it was spitting now, this evening, in waning September. She wouldn't comment. She wouldn't sigh. It would pass, like it always did. Hopefully sooner rather than later.

Lynn lived in a tall, narrow townhouse at the top of the hill that dominated the oldest, most inward-looking neighborhood of the city. The house had commanded that spot, skeletal and imperious, for centuries. And Lynn's family had inhabited it, cloistered and reclusive, for the same amount of time. Watching from its great height as the witches were hanged, three hundred fifty years ago, in the field across the road. Watching the soldiers massacre one another in the same field, two hundred fifty years ago—fighting out some arcane dispute over trade tariffs. Watching the factory workers and the students immolate themselves one hundred fifty years ago and fifty years ago, respectively. It all made Lynn tired.

The field had since been converted into a public park where rats and children rode in plastic boats shaped like waterfowl. And the telescope with which her ancestors had observed their surroundings—new enough in the early days to be satanic, though they'd known to keep their counsel—had long since disappeared. The invisible and now empty cupboard in which they'd hidden the device still made Lynn smile when she had cause to visit the third floor.

Family lore, unskillfully plagiarized, was that the patriarch of their line, a hanging judge of the old school, had brought a curse upon the heads of his descendants by not only ridding the town of its witches, but accumulating the property those witches had left behind for his own nefarious purposes. Though, admittedly, neither Lynn nor any of her relatives of the previous generations had noticed a particularly malign influence on their fortunes. Granted, Lynn was the last of the line—and, at the age of forty-five, likely to remain so. But that was more a product of boredom than of cruel and rigid fate twisting back on itself. Most of her family simply couldn't be bothered to make the effort.

Moreover, though they continued to inhabit the gaunt house across the centuries—again, largely the result of inertia—they'd ceased to care about the "line" *per se* six or seven generations ago. As a rule, Lynn's people valued capability over birth. Hence her mother's successful turn as a trial lawyer. Hence her grandfather's forays into unnecessary amateur accountancy (he'd wisely left the family's fortunes to the professionals). Hence Brendan.

She risked another glance across the table. He'd tipped his bread roll onto the floor, where he was now grinding it to sticky crumbs under a bare foot. Though perhaps Brendan was a bit of a stretch. Formerly the boy who sold her cigarettes at the corner store, he'd caught her eye four years previously, just after the last remaining relative who might object to him—a dotty, demented uncle (though he'd been dotty and demented at the age of thirty as well)—had died three months before. And so, on a whim, Lynn had married the boy. He was twenty years her junior and, she suspected, illiterate, but she didn't care. She liked the waiflike way in which he looked at her.

Also, she could sense that Brendan was not, by nature, manipulative. He was clearly fond of her, and she'd been pleased by his shy and startled reaction to her proposal. Even after he'd told her that he was an unwise choice as a life partner, that he had problems, a troubled history–something about a squat and a predatory choreographer–she'd found him charming. And now that he was hers, she liked to listen to him recount the tales of his disturbing past. She didn't pay them any attention, of course. She simply enjoyed the wistful expression that flickered over his face as he recounted the horrors. Encouraging him to talk.

The eating difficulties, however, had been a surprise. Having always considered anorexia a privilege of her own class, Lynn hadn't expected that sort of behavior from her new husband. The background in dance, she supposed. And though she was grateful to Brendan for opening her mind–she hated to think of herself as narrow–she was nonplussed by the violence of the changes that came over him when he was in the throes of his condition.

For it wasn't only his eating habits that altered at these times. His personality as a whole became hostile, secretive, and withdrawn. So extreme was the atmosphere he created about himself that it seemed to Lynn to affect the world outside. Leaving the streets and the parks, the river and the gardens, grey, damp, and wet. Fanciful, of course, but such was her impression.

The compulsive little habits that Lynn enjoyed—and facilitated—in Brendan also became disturbing and even dangerous when the eating difficulties were upon him. Brendan, for example, spent much of his time, ill or well, collecting small dog and cat figurines—a hobby he'd brought with him from his days at the corner store. The eight or nine animals that had once lined the glass barrier between Lynn and the cigarettes, in fact, had been carefully and dutifully moved from their place in the public eye to the mantlepiece of the marble hearth in her great-grandfather's study once Brendan had taken possession of the room.

Though that hadn't lasted. Irritated more than she'd imagined she would be by the sight of the sentimental, brightly colored figurines arrayed across the three-hundred year old piece of wood that her great- great-grandfather had brought back from an ill-fated journey to Argentina to serve as said mantlepiece, she'd suggested to Brendan that he devote a separate room entirely to his collection of animals. She certainly had enough to spare—rooms, that is. And then he might leave the study to, well, the things one does in a study.

To her relief, Brendan had acquiesced quietly, and Lynn had been pleased to peek into the disused former morning room once or twice every week to observe his growing collection. His flourishing collection. Unchecked now that he was funded.

But when his mood soured, Brendan was less accommodating. First, he would purchase many more of the little cats and dogs than he did otherwise. Not that Lynn begrudged him the money, of course. She'd have settled even more on him if he'd only diversify his interests. Rather, it was the obsessive and, again, secretive quality of his mode of consumption at these moments. Once, she'd even seen him scuttling into the morning room with a large plastic sack full of the things hidden under a badly buttoned coat. As though she'd ever question him or protest.

But still worse than the increased rate of his consumption was that he no longer adhered to the prohibition against the figurines leaving the morning room. As hours passed on the bad days, those days when he hadn't eaten for a week or more, Lynn would stumble across the miniature cats and dogs in every corner of the house—the kitchen, her own writing room, the piano room, even lined up in twos or threes in the hall. Whence she'd collect them in a cardboard box to return to the morning room. Only to find them ranging about the house again a few hours later.

After discovering one stuffed into her pillow case—like a cockroach in a bad dream—she'd vowed to dispose of them, all of them, herself. But an hour or so later, she'd calmed. She couldn't do that to Brendan. And besides, she was by no means unfamiliar with eccentricity. She'd had four hundred years of epigenetic conditioning to appreciate his oddities. Thus, she simply waited for the spell to pass.

As she was doing now. On this dark evening at the end of a particularly bad September. She finished her halibut and gazed across the table at him. He'd smashed his own into a yellowish paste that he was now shaping into a narrow structure at the center of his plate.

"You aren't eating?" she finally asked him. Her voice light and encouraging. The voice one uses with the mentally ill.

"I don't want you to watch me." He used his fork, with some violence now, to flatten the tower of paste into a thin coating that obscured the plate's tasteful floral pattern.

"I needn't watch you," she said, still bright, pushing back her chair and standing. "I can easily leave you alone–"

He scrambled to his feet and snatched his plate from the table. "I'll eat it in the morning room."

Then, after glaring at her for five or six seconds, he turned and ran from the room, shouting back at her: "don't watch!"

"I really don't think I want to watch," she murmured to herself as she followed a minute later, giving him sufficient time to slam the door.

Something, she determined, must be done.

THE next day, Lynn resolved to speak seriously–maternally, she thought, despite herself–to Brendan about the cats and the dogs. If not about his more serious problems. The previous night, she'd discovered an orange plastic collie at the bottom of the cup in which she kept her toothbrush, and in her surprise, she'd nearly dropped it—the toothbrush—into the toilet. Moreover, she'd woken at two in the morning to the sound of what she was certain were living cats or dogs sliding or clicking across the floor of the room above her. The room housing his collection. And if Brendan was now smuggling stray—living—animals into her house, she'd be forced to exert her authority. Wrapping herself in her mother's silk dressing gown, she prepared to do battle.

She met Brendan in the breakfast room as he was pouring himself a cup of coffee. A good sign. Cereal would have been better, but coffee was an improvement. He nodded at her, wary, when she settled herself into a chair across from him. But otherwise, he didn't speak.

When he was suffering from one of his moods, Brendan slept in the morning room rather than in their bedroom. An arrangement that suited Lynn well, both because she didn't relish the thought of sharing a bed with someone as clearly unstable as Brendan was when he wasn't eating, and also because she'd been single long enough to appreciate a bed of her own. Despite the sound of the clicking paws that had disturbed her sleep last night, she was feeling sharp and energetic now. She glanced out the window. Also despite the weather, which looked to be gearing up for an unprecedented storm.

"I heard the dogs," she said, pouring her own cup of coffee.

He frowned. "What dogs?"

"Cats, then."

"Where?"

"In the morning room." She sipped from the cup. "How many have you got up there?"

"I haven't counted," he replied slowly. "A few thousand, I think."

"No, not the figurines." She crushed her irritation at what she knew was his deliberate refusal to understand her. "The living dogs and cats. I heard them running about up there. One barked."

"I don't think so." His expression was baffled. Almost concerned on her behalf.

"Don't be silly–" she began.

"I can show you," he interrupted. "Come up and look now."

Still irritated, Lynn chose to call his bluff. She knew he'd expected her to decline. But his calm denial of what she was confident she'd heard the night before was more than she could tolerate.

Grabbing her coffee, she stood. "Fine. Let's go now."

They walked together, almost companionable, up the wide, wooden stairway, past the paintings of Lynn's cadaverous ancestors, until they reached the third-floor corridor. Blushing, Brendan bent to retrieve a tiny jade cat–nicer, Lynn thought, than many of his others–that was lurking to the side of a balustrade. Then he walked a few more paces and pushed open the door to the morning room.

Though the room was menacing—every surface covered with figurines, all staring or simpering in the direction of the door—it was also clear from the moment they entered that no living animal was present. The floor, at least the bits of it that weren't occupied by plastic, resin, or ceramic, was unmarked. There was no fur or hair on the furniture. There was no movement. The lack of movement, in fact, added to the sinister air.

Brendan's plate from last night, Lynn noticed, had been licked clean and tossed onto an old rocking chair. Absentmindedly, she collected it to return to the kitchen. In the same part of her mind, she noted that the rain that had been threatening earlier was now upon them. Huge drops were hurling themselves against the window, inches away from a parade of Persian cats in improbable hues, arrayed across the windowsill.

"I see I was mistaken," she finally said. Always willing to concede an error. "I apologize, Brendan."

"Don't," he replied. "I know I can be—difficult—at times. I'm lucky to have you."

He made as if to kiss her, but she shook her head, smiling. Uninterested in obligation. "I'm the lucky one." Then she turned to go. "Take as long as you need to work through this. But do let me know whether there's anything I can do to help? Anything at all?"

"I will, Lynn." He dropped his eyes to his bare feet. "I think it's passing. Just a few more days."

UNFORTUNATELY, it wasn't passing. In fact, that night was even worse than the night before. Though it was possible, Lynn confessed to herself as she prepared for bed, that her own mood had been unduly affected by the raging storm that had continued unabated now for twelve hours. The damp electric air that moved in eddies up and down the staircase of the brittle house was enough to drive anyone in a paranoiac direction—even one, such as herself, who'd been bred to it. She was impressed by—and proud of—Brendan for retaining what remained of his equilibrium in the face of the building's atmosphere. Smug, she congratulated herself on choosing well.

When she flicked on the bathroom light, however, wanting to clean her teeth for the night, her self-congratulatory mood evaporated. In the wavering glow—waxing and waning in the storm—she surveyed a scene that she'd not have believed possible four years before. An abnormal scene. A compulsive scene.

Hundreds of tiny dog and cat figurines. Filling both sinks. Scattered into the corners. Stacked in layers on the floor of both the tub and the shower. All staring, vacant and saccharine, in her direction.

Without speaking, she backed out of the room, marched down to the kitchen, and retrieved a plastic bin bag. Then, having stomped back up the stairs, she swept them all into the bag. Tying the top in a double knot, she left the lumpen mess in the corner. She'd dispose of it tomorrow. Along with an additional bag of whichever of their compatriots remained on the loose. A line had been crossed.

Having reached her decision and slipped into bed, however, sleep eluded her. The lightning was just random enough to intrude itself into her consciousness–both when it lit up the sky and, as she waited tensely for the next bolt, when it didn't. The sound of the rain pounding on her windows felt sentient–needy and demanding. Angry specifically with her.

And above all, she brooded on her fear that ridding the house of the cats and dogs would also rid it of Brendan. She didn't want to lose him. But she also could no longer live with the figurines. A practical person, Lynn shrank from emotional impasses such as the one that currently faced her. For hours, she twisted about in her sheets, unable to settle into a comfortable position.

Moreover, when she finally did slip into unconsciousness, she was troubled by nightmares of the sort that hadn't plagued her since her childhood. Nightmares sufficiently appalling to launch her, repeatedly, into a shaking state of semi-awareness. Paralyzed between two, equally harrowing, mental states.

It was in one of these in-between states that Lynn spotted the cats. Two of them at the foot of her bed, their eyes glowing in the sporadic lightning. Watching her.

True, they weren't feral, aggressive, or menacing. Indeed, they moved–when they did move–with a quiet docility, seeking affection. But when she saw their eyes and then felt their small paws picking their way over her covers, she sat straight up in bed and shrieked. After that, she shrieked a second time.

No one answered. No one came. Though the cats, after a moment of frozen rigidity, leapt, as cats will, from her bed to the ground. Trotting, affronted, out the door. No longer deigning to notice her.

Lynn, never one to cower when she could fight, threw off her covers, grabbed a brass candlestick that some long-dead aunt had left beside the bed for that purpose, and followed. In maddened pursuit. She'd find them. She'd put them out. Never mind the rain, the lightning, and the storm. They would not occupy her house.

As she passed through the door, however, she paused, confused. A scampering clicking was reaching her from the direction of the stairs. Not a cat. Too loud and ungainly for a cat. A small dog, she guessed. The size, perhaps, of a pug.

Slowing, yet still wielding the candlestick, she neared the bottom step. Where she saw what were now three shadowed forms. Two cats flowing up to the third floor with a liquid grace. And a fat dog gamboling up behind them.

Eager, she leapt at them. But when she reached the foot of the stairs, she tripped and landed face-forward on the thin carpet. The candlestick rolling away into the darkness. In silence, she cursed. And then she winced.

For her fall had been a spectacular one. Painful. Something, she could already tell, was now severely wrong with her wrist. But bewildered as to how she could have mistaken a step that she'd negotiated in the dark from the time she could walk, she ignored the throbbing pain. Instead, extending her uninjured hand in the direction of her feet, she sought out the brass candlestick.

The candlestick eluded her. Indeed, rather than encountering anything as comforting brass, her hand fell upon a disquieting mound of plastic, resin, and ceramic. Insinuating itself between her fingers. A substantial mound. Piled up at the base of the stair.

Hastily, she drew back her arm. Overcome by a sudden, violent nausea. She couldn't have been more disgusted if she'd reached blindly into mass of insects or rodents. On the verge of tears now, she curled her feet up closer to her stomach. She didn't want any part of her body anywhere near the mass of objects.

After perhaps ten minutes of immobility on the stairs, however, Lynn began to feel ashamed of herself. This was her house. These were her stairs. And though she was obviously in no state now, injured, past midnight, in the midst of a violent storm, to assert her jurisdiction over the place, she would damned well do so tomorrow. By noon, the things would be gone. As would Brendan. Yes, fine, she liked him. But he was no longer worth the trouble.

On her way back to her bedroom, she noticed that the bin bag she'd left in the corner of the bathroom near the shower was shredded to pieces and empty. But she paid it no attention. She'd take action tomorrow. Tonight she needed rest.

BRENDAN and his belongings were not, as it turned out, gone by noon the next day. But that was only because he didn't show himself until dinner. Wan and ill, he sat in his customary place, gazing across the table at Lynn, who was spoiling for a confrontation. Even his delicate fragility did nothing for her. She wanted him gone. Though, she mused to herself as she took a steely sip of her wine, at least the rain had let up for a few hours. A watery moonbeam even shone through the tall window.

"Not eating?" She fixed him with a cold stare as he failed to ingest the risotto sitting in front of him.

He shook his head.

"Brendan," she announced, "it's long past time that we—"

He stood and took up his plate. "I'll eat in the morning room. Don't watch."

Stupefied, Lynn stared after him as he left the room. And then, overcome by rage—a new emotion for her—she pushed back her chair and stood. In her own house. The boy was treating her like some disposable piece of clutter in her very own house. It was unacceptable.

She slammed her napkin down on the table, circled his chair, and strode out of the room behind him. Don't watch, indeed. The lunatic was likely feeding the food—*her* food—to his filthy animals.

But when she reached the closed door of the morning room, Lynn re-thought her determination to surprise and humiliate him. As a rule, she was neither an angry nor a vindictive person. Both states demanded more energy than she was prepared to expend on ephemeral interpersonal interactions. She couldn't remember the last time she'd entertained either.

Moreover, and perhaps more importantly, she felt bound to uphold her earlier promises to Brendan regarding his privacy and his independence—even if he himself was now failing spectacularly to fulfill his own side of their bargain. She was honorable. He was not. But the disparity should scarcely surprise her. There was no need to push their relationship to a breaking point over an issue she ought to have seen coming four years before. Having taken up the boy from the corner store. What other outcome could she have expected?

A muted growling, and then the sound of scuffling paws on the other side of the door, however, re-ignited her rage. Honor could only serve a person so long and so well. Her situation had become untenable, and something—dishonorable even—must be done. For the sake of the house, if nothing else. Autocratic, much like the house, Lynn pushed open the door.

And stared.

The room was much the same as it had been when she and Brendan had visited the day before. The animals. The dinner plate. The rocking chair. The rain spattered across the windows.

Except that now, the tiny, immobile figurine animals had been replaced by hundreds, thousands, of writhing and squirming full-sized cats and dogs. Pawing and climbing over one another, whining, snuffling, and mewing. And every one of them, despite its obvious discomfort in the seething clot of bodies, was gazing in her direction. Evaluating her. Judging her.

Brendan himself was turned partially away, facing the larger portion of the animals. But she could nonetheless see what he was doing. Even if she no longer wanted to. Having removed his shirt, he'd exposed his chest, shoulders, and arms, which were as perfect as they'd ever been.

But there was also a hole in the small of his back, the size and color of the interior of a melon, which was slavering and drooling over the dinner plate he'd removed from the dining room. She could see it distinctly. Devouring the risotto he was spooning into it. And the scraps that the hole in his back failed to ingest, that it dropped in its eagerness, were being gobbled up by the cats and dogs closest to his feet. Even as they continued to goggle up at Lynn.

Lynn, her hand on the door, turned to the side and vomited. Three Manx cats pounced on the puddle and began to lick it up. And the rain fell harder. Pounding against the window.

Brendan, who had turned, startled, at the sound of her entry, now smiled at her, apologetic instead, and stepped toward the door. Pushed it closed. Then he set the half-consumed plate of risotto on the rocking chair, where a dachshund snuffled into it with a pointed nose.

"I told you not to watch," he told her. Unnecessarily.

She tried to back away, but he was still holding the door shut. She stopped. Frozen.

"I'm sorry–" he began.

Coming to herself, Lynn held up an angry hand. And interrupted him. It was time for him to leave. Long past time. She cared not a whit for his apologies or explanations.

All that emerged when she opened her mouth, however, were a series of growling moans punctuated by a small yip. Perplexed, she dropped her hand and tried again. Three loud barks. And a whine. She clapped both hands over her mouth. Moaned again.

And then, peering at Brendan, she stiffened. Aghast at the realization that he was entirely unsurprised by the state of her voice–that, in some way, he'd expected it. Giving in to her despair, she began to weep instead.

The noise that she made was a whining howl. Un-human. A sound not replicable by a human. A number of the dogs, however, still watching her, joined in, matching her tone precisely. And a handful of the cats tilted their heads in her direction.

Brendan held up his own hand now to stop her. But she refused to quiet herself. And so, shrugging, he spoke over her. "As I said, you shouldn't have watched. And I am sorry about this."

Most of the dogs in the room were now yelping and clamoring along with Lynn. Brendan raised his voice further. "But it isn't as bad as it seems, Lynn. Really. I'll care for you." He frowned. "You know, when I'm not working."

The rain was sluicing down the windows like a cataract. Brendan nodded in its direction. "As you can see, things bog down a bit in the autumn."

He put his arm around her shoulders and held her to him as she shuddered and yelped. "But truly, Lynn, do let me know whether there's anything I can do to help? Anything at all?"

Light and encouraging. The voice one uses with mentally ill people.

Lynn and the dogs continued to howl.

Fog

TWELVE unsharpened pencils, two floppy disks from the mid-1990s, a Twinkie of indeterminate age—though he believed they stopped producing them at least five years ago—a post-it note from around the same era as the floppy disks, reminding him to attend his divorce proceedings, and a snow globe featuring the theatre that burned to the ground a few months before. Philip dumped it all into the shoebox and settled the lid on top. He was one week away from retirement. He had one unsettled case—a case that had dogged him from his earliest days on the force. He feared that the cliché would kill him.

His continued interest in the case was, after all, unseemly. At best. He had little to no chance of breaking it before taking his shoebox and heading home—and his insistence on attempting to do so smacked of the compulsive, if not the absurd. To him as well as to his mostly tolerant, very much younger, colleagues. But if he didn't at least try now that his time was coming to an end—be his persistence ever so neurotic—he'd never forgive himself. He'd dwell on it forever, as he cared for his pitcher plants or plucked at his guitar strings or whatever else he'd being doing to fill his protracted, hollow, retired days. He'd be trapped with the incomplete oddity of the thing eternally. And he didn't want to begin his new life in that way, especially not in a wretched month like October. October was always the worst for him. The case had begun in an October. More than three decades ago, now.

And it *was* a strange case. Fraud and market manipulation. Not his strength, as he was the first to admit—having made his reputation later, over the ensuing decades, in Vice and then in Homicide. But he'd been new to the force at the time, and the investigative team had needed an additional body. He'd been available. Eager to prove himself.

They'd told him to stay in the background, and he had, because though fraud was as old as commerce, subtle market manipulation of the sort that had come to his superiors' attention was new at the time, nearly forty years ago. They hadn't wanted to take ill-conceived steps. They hadn't wanted to fuck up.

And indeed, they hadn't. Within a month of initiating their investigation, the team had identified a suspect. Within two months, they'd convinced one another that their suspect was guilty. But they'd never gathered sufficient evidence to convince a prosecutor. They'd scarcely gathered evidence at all. Slipping as the material persistently did through both actual and figurative fingers.

Additionally, though they shrank from expressing it to one another, their suspect, *as* a suspect, posed a problem. A lone actor rather than a cartel or an association, she was, moreover, a youngish woman. A girl, really. And at the time—forty years ago—the youth and, well, the femininity of the suspect had left certain members of the team uncomfortable. Not that any had balked at performing his duties, of course. But everyone, including Philip, would have been happier had they been cornering a collection of fat, greedy, duplicitous men. Sexist, perhaps, but Philip was old, and he was willing to accept the epithet.

In hindsight, the team's scruples hadn't mattered. Not only did they fail to collect sufficient evidence to indict the girl, but the witnesses they gathered to identify her and to soil her character proved entirely unreliable. All were undoubtedly describing the same girl when they made their statements. But all remembered her in different ways. Most were unable even to identify her in a photograph. Though, granted, the photographs the team had accumulated were blurry. Some little more than a grey mist.

As months, and then years, had passed, the team assigned to the case had become less and less reluctant to exert pressure on the girl—or even to resort to questionable practices in cobbling together material to pursue an indictment. Her femininity had become a provocation to them rather than a font of protective impulses. Taunting them as the girl continued, endlessly, to confound them. Still sexist, if in a slightly more pernicious way.

But regardless of their changing and hardening attitudes, none of their strategies had succeeded. If anything, their suspect had become only more elusive the harder they'd pushed her. Disappearing for days or weeks on end. Befuddling their growing collection of witnesses. Only to reappear in the form of an inexplicable crash or bubble a few months later. Before dissipating once more.

Until finally, three years into the case, its lead investigator had altered the team's approach. Tackling their suspect head on, he'd determined, was a non-starter. But they might bring her in on a series of minor charges and work from there. Treat her, in fact, like a cartel. Less an individual than an amorphous accumulation of energy.

Those who'd managed to tail her for more than a few hours at a time had all reported similar, and similarly remarkable, patterns of behavior from her. As much as the girl enjoyed throwing global markets into confusion, for example she also fancied petty pilfering. Shoplifting. Extracting wallets from handbags. Exhibiting a skill, according to those who'd seen it in action, that rivalled the most hardened of street professionals. No one saw her coming. No one saw her leave. And all that remained in her wake was emptiness. They could work with that.

When Philip, the youngest of the team, was transferred from the case in its fifth year, in due course finding himself in Homicide, the investigation was still counting on trapping the girl on a shoplifting or larceny charge. Moreover, and perhaps surprisingly, as the older members of the team retired and died, the strategy taken on by those few who replaced them remained the same. It likewise remained utterly unsuccessful.

Thus, over the decades, the crashes and the bubbles—sufficiently distinctive, trademarked even, that the girl may as well have appended her portrait to them—continued unabated. The girl herself, unchecked. The energy accumulating. While Philip, traumatized by those first five years on the force, saved his own money in carefully ordered shoeboxes under his shed.

IN now this final week of his career, however, he wanted to try his luck with the girl once more. Take one last shot at her. He knew that she was still working—the market had taken one of her signature plunges only days before. And reports of her appearances continued to fill a file that remained open and dutifully maintained—though it had never quite made the jump from a physical to a digital object. Only two days ago, he'd read, perusing the aging folder, which still smelled of frustrated, decades-old cigarette smoke, she'd been spotted hovering about the public clock in the financial district. Spooking passing investors. Saturating the place with her disorderly presence.

Philip would begin there. He shifted the shoebox he'd taken to carrying along with him now that his desk had been reassigned, and started off. Recognizing his quixotic persistence for what it was, but determined nonetheless. He must—*must*—try.

When he reached his destination, he blinked, surprised. If he'd been the sort to smile, he would have smiled. It was as though the girl had been waiting for him. Indeed, as he neared the clock with its thin skirt of patchy greenery and its three scrolled benches, never used, he felt very much like she was deliberately displaying to him her still familiar form.

Wan and grey, squeezed to the edge of one of the benches, she was feeding the plague-ridden pigeons from a paper sack she'd balanced precariously on one knee. Wearing something thin, trailing, and knitted. After emptying the sack, she dropped it to the ground and stood. Flicking a quick glance in his direction.

Philip froze. Littering? He considered. And then he chastised himself. No. He'd need something a bit more than that to make headway with the prosecutor. Besides, the sack, his evidence, was already gone. Scooped up with unexpected violence by a stray puff of wind. Disposed of, after all.

Clutching his shoebox, he moved closer to her. The girl, sensing his interest—and having for a split second solicited it (or so he felt)—appeared not to care at all whether he followed. Nebulous and unmethodical, she began walking out of the financial district and into the green space that separated it from the University campus. Cutting a swath through the bankers who nervously stepped to the side as she approached them. Pretending not to see her. Unable, it appeared, to see her. Though one stumbled, tripping, into a gutter. As if momentarily blinded.

Feeling a trifle foolish, Philip trailed her. She moved with the muted grace of a dancer. Or the ghost of a dancer. An uncanny grace. A grace, in fact, that he could just remember, now that he thought about it, from three decades before. He couldn't see her feet under the complicated knit ensemble she'd wrapped around her body, which leant her more than ever the air of a distracted phantom. And gradually, he found himself feeling the enchantment that had troubled the team in the early days of their investigation.

But when she paused, bored, outside the walls of the defunct chocolate company–walls that were nearly opaque now under the weight of the political graffiti disfiguring the glass–Philip set aside his wistful interest and sharpened his attention. The building, vulnerable, would appeal to her larcenous instincts. And indeed, with a small smile, she approached the mud-encrusted entryway, paused for a split second, pulled open the door, and entered.

Philip lingered outside, nonplussed. Uncertain as to how to proceed. The chocolate company was a public and commercial building.

And he'd seen for himself that the door had been unlocked (he'd expected her to have to force it). All of which meant that she had as much right to enter it as he had. There was little he could do other than wait. Observe what she picked up inside.

But when she exited a few minutes later, all she'd collected was a chocolate bar, which she delicately unwrapped and sampled. He frowned in vexation. As everyone in the city knew, they were giving the stuff away for free. Philip himself wouldn't have touched it. Afflicted by the same scruples that had tormented him from his first days on the force. But the girl's failure to boycott an unethical consumer product was hardly criminal. At least, not yet.

Discouraged, he followed her further. And a half hour later—after a desultory stroll along the river, where cold and unhappy children were capsizing in sailing dinghies while their parents took photos—she arrived at the Vogel. Slumping down onto a bench across the street, less well-maintained than those in the financial district, Philip held his shoebox in his lap. Not troubling even to watch her enter the cuckoo-clock monstrosity. Increasingly provoked.

There was nothing to steal from the Vogel. Heaven alone knew why she'd chosen to visit it. And when, a few minutes after the girl had entered the establishment, he saw a small man with a hat and a huge erection exit it, he stared down at the box in his hands, questioning his determination to pursue the case. Bitter and angry at his ongoing failure. Bitter and angry at his pointless career. *Not* criminal, he muttered to himself, glancing up at the little man. The man politely raised his hat. Though it ought to be.

Forty-five minutes later, the girl left the Vogel—the museum was striking the hour with its usual frenzied thoroughness—and strode, now with more purpose, in the direction of the old hill that had dominated the the city since the latter's founding. Philip jumped to his feet. Optimistic once more. If he was lucky, she'd be tempted by one of the decrepit mansions that lined the crest. They weren't her style, true. But nor, would he have thought, was shoplifting from a charity shop. And yet, he'd read the file...

But the girl, as he'd half expected, refused to perform for him—merely climbing, still fluid, still ethereal, to the top of the hill, where she paused for thirty or forty seconds. Philip, breathing hard, tripped over a wet pug dog as he followed on her heels. Cursing under his breath.

As he'd begun to notice in the financial district—though the effect was more pronounced here, in this neighborhood, where anything beyond the ritualized ordinary was a source of quiet disapproval—the girl elicited no attention from those whom she passed. If anything, she inspired negative attention. And this notwithstanding her unusual appearance: the trailing knit, the absent feet. She was invisible to those who encountered her.

Philip alone watched her. Targeted her. The others flowed past her like water. Frowning, he redoubled his concentration. The girl's odd effect only made him more determined. There *was* something criminal about her. There had to be. Criminality was the only explanation for her influence on the crowd.

Having gazed out over the city for a little less than a minute, the girl moved, now with even greater speed back down the hill, in the direction of the public park. When she reached the street that separated it from the old neighborhood, she crossed without waiting for the light. And as Philip crossed after her, trotting, ignoring the angry screech of a taxi braking to keep from running him over, he saw her moving toward the dock where the city stored its plastic waterfowl boats. Unpopular in October, but still available on sunny afternoons for the more intrepid tourist. The sun was setting, he noted vaguely, and the rats were out. The attraction was closed.

As he gained on the girl, the darkness gathered about them both with greater insistence, such that he could scarcely see her. She was visible to him now as nothing more than a motionless column of haze at the foot the low bridge that connected the mainland to the pier. Wavering in and out of perceptibility. Less prominent, in fact, than the rats, which, like the bankers before them, had parted for her in a river of smoke as they swarmed from the cooler water beyond the pier to the warmer water near the mainland. A nightly performance unseen by the daylight tourists.

Despite the dim light, however, Philip could still see her well enough to ascertain what happened next. Though the attraction had been closed for over an hour, and though signs warning against approaching the boats without a ticket or permission adorned several posts along the bridge, the girl strode to the nearest of the craft, stepped onto it, and cast off. Disregarding the signs. Disregarding propriety or property rights. Acting as though she owned the vehicle.

She was stealing a waterfowl boat. A crime. Philip had her.

Seizing his chance, he sprinted over the pier, leapt across the moored craft, and landed with a wobble in the girl's boat. Pleased by his agility, given his advanced age. And then, strict and severe, he sat in the plastic seat across from her and addressed her.

"The attraction," he said, "is closed, miss."

"Yes," she agreed.

"It's a criminal offence to tamper with the boats after closing hours."

"It is," she said gravely.

"I'm afraid that I must ask you to accompany me to the station."

Rather than answering, the girl let her eyes stray across the black water. Stagnant even in October. Rippling with rats, but little else that was living.

Philip, following her gaze, cleared his throat. "That is, once we've returned to shore."

Worried, he glanced down at the bottom of the boat. He believed that one maneuvered it by peddling. Though in his almost forty years on the force, he'd never once had occasion to experiment. He pushed a cautious toe against the plastic footpad. Nothing happened.

"What's in your box," she asked after an awkward minute had passed.

"Oh," he said. Embarrassed. Though it ought to have been the girl who was blushing in the darkness. He lifted the lid, and a breeze made off with the post-it note. The rest remained in place. "Floppy disks, a Twinkie, and a snow globe."

She bent toward him and lifted the snow globe out of the box. Gently, as though it were a great treasure. Then she smiled as she tilted it backward and forward.

"It's pretty," she commented. "I miss the theatre. Someone ought to steal that idiot's axe."

"Theft is illegal," he replied.

"Yes," she agreed again. She didn't return the snow globe.

Philip felt a stronger breeze begin to move the boat further away from the shore. And a current that he'd not have expected on the small, shallow pond. Waves that were more than rats rippling. He gripped the sides of the boat.

Then, thinking he ought to begin moving the situation toward its appropriate conclusion, he resecured his shoebox, absent the snow globe, and settled his feet more firmly on the pedals at the bottom of the boat. Furrowing his brow, he pushed them through three or four cycles. Nothing happened.

The girl, trailing the fingertips of one hand in the water, gazed across at him. "What are you doing?"

The boat had begun to tilt and right itself in what were now rollers. Waves that couldn't possibly have formed in the pond. He wasn't certain they'd even have formed in the toxic bay beyond the viaduct. Also, the air was cleaner. Saltier. No longer stagnant.

And he could see nothing around them.

A prickle of fear spread across the back of Philip's neck. "Where are we?"

"I don't know," the girl replied, still grave.

He peered beyond her. Black. Night had fallen. Dusk was gone. He couldn't even make out urban lights. A shore. Any shore. Twisting back, he gazed behind him. Nothing. Possibly mist.

"Here's your snow globe," she said, holding it out to him. Apologetic. An attempt to alter his mood.

Without speaking, he took it and replaced it in the shoebox. Secured the lid a third time. Rubbed his hands together. The October air was affecting him. As it always did. He began to shiver.

And then, as he stared across the boat at the girl, realization hit. He'd been working on the fraud case for close to forty years. His entire adult life. And he knew that he had the culprit sitting across from him in this boat. But she was no older now than she'd been when he'd joined the force. A girl. A child, almost. The sort to provoke an embarrassed guilt, at least in the beginning, in the craggier, less enlightened cops who'd introduced him to his craft.

She snuggled down into her knit wrap and smiled at him. And then, low and earnest, she spoke. "Thank you, Philip."

He found his voice. "Why?"

"No one notices me. No one has ever noticed me. I can't remember the last time I was seen." She closed her eyes, luxuriating in the cold air on her skin. "Except for you. You see me."

He held the shoebox tightly to his chest and huddled at the bottom of the boat. Shaking. Unable to respond.

"Thank you," she repeated.

And the boat moved swiftly in the black, invisible current. Through the fog and the mist. Going nowhere.

Wind

"SO, what are you going to do about it?"

This from the largest of the boys. He was holding Bolon's rucksack by one strap, swinging it around his head. Snickering. "We needed a bag. You had one. Now it's ours."

Bolon stood silent, gazing at the boy, deferential but not excessively so, trying not to provoke further aggression. His aunt had told him to avoid the shortcut home. But the conventional route not only took him past the remains of the City Theatre, which spooked him, but was twice as long.

Besides which, he neither liked nor trusted his aunt. His guardian now for three years, since his parents had died in the accident. A twist of black cloth abandoned on the expressway flattened across their windscreen by a stray gust of air. Bolon had been waiting for them to collect him from his sailing lesson on the river. Since then, to the extent that he could, he contravened every directive, even the tiniest, that his aunt set down.

The boy, sensing that Bolon wasn't reacting, slowed the momentum of the rucksack and then lowered it to the ground between his feet. After that, he grinned at his followers. An assortment of eleven other boys, ranging between the ages of nine and fifteen. At twelve, Bolon fit well among them. Though he wasn't one of them. Not yet.

When Bolon still failed to respond, the boy advanced on him, belligerent now, and repeated his question. "So, what are you going to do about it?"

As a rush of anger surged up inside of him, unsummoned and unwelcome, a breeze scattered a spray of misshapen, rusting bolts over the boys. They and Bolon were gathered, illegally, under the abandoned viaduct construction site–having crawled, Bolon first, the boys sneaking after him, through a hole in the chain-link fence. The bolts had fallen from a tower of disused scaffolding to the side of their altercation. Distressed, Bolon squinted up at the grey November sky.

"What the fuck?" The large boy's second, Bolon suspected. Fourteen, perhaps, but solid and menacing with adult fat and muscle. Picking a stray bolt out of the collar of his turquoise hoodie and pondering it.

Bolon, wanting to draw their attention away from the breeze–and the bolts–decided to speak. In desperation rather than in hope. "Why do you need a bag?"

"Need*ed*," the first boy emphasized, once again on familiar ground. He held up the rucksack. "Not anymore. Now we've got one. Now *you* need one." The other boys laughed.

Bolon licked his lips. He didn't want to become angry again. Bad things happened when he became angry. His parents had been late that day, leaving him, as he'd thought, stranded alone at the sailing school, and he'd felt the rage building inside of him then too–

"Why *did* you need a bag?" He was babbling. This conversation was useless. But anything was better than yelling. Giving in to his emotions.

The boys smirked at one another. "And who the fuck are you to ask me anything?" The largest was beginning to enjoy himself again.

"Does it have to be my bag?"

"*Does it have to be my bag*?" The brawny one. Taunting. "Why? Will you find us another one?"

"I might," Bolon temporized. "What sort do you want? I mean, if not my rucksack?"

"You ask a lot of questions." The leader ran his eyes over the other boys. "Let's go. We've got what we came for."

They began walking–strutting–in the direction of the hole in the fence. Swinging Bolon's rucksack. And then tossing it back and forth in an impromptu, lazy sort of rugby formation.

Bolon, after a few seconds of indecision trotted after them.

"Wait," he said. "At least let me come with you."

"Go home, little boy." The largest didn't deign to look back at him.

"I don't want to go home." Bolon was breathing heavily. "I haven't got a home." He didn't know why he was lying to them.

The large boy stopped. Then he turned, slowly, back toward Bolon. Drawing out the moment. Still smirking. "We're bringing the bag to Cardina. You want to meet her?"

"Who's Cardina?"

"She feeds us."

"Oh." Bolon realized that he was hungry. "Yes. Yes, I'd like to meet her."

The boy shrugged, turned away, and resumed strolling toward the hole in the fence. The others trailed behind. And last of all came Bolon.

THE boys lived not far from the viaduct. And less than five minutes after they'd made their way through the fence, they reached a disused factory with a decrepit "Vogel Chemicals" sign teetering on the verge of collapse above massive steel doors that had been bent backward and open as though assaulted by some impossible wind. The boys drifted through the doorway as though they owned the place. Which, to an extent, they did.

But just before passing under the sign, Bolon stopped, his head up, feeling eyes on him. Anxious. And then, after a few seconds of confusion, he saw it: a spotless dark sedan with tinted windows idling at an intersection. His heart began thumping hard in his chest.

The oldest boy, who'd noticed Bolon's interest, grabbed his arm and pulled him along, shaking his head. "You keep out of the way of that guy, if you know what's good for you."

"Why?" Bolon narrowed his eyes, trying to get a better view of the occupant of the car, but all he could see was a small rivulet of black smoke escaping from a crack in the driver's side window.

"He's looking for dancers," the boy said. "A bad scene." And then, when Bolon's expression didn't change: "you want money, Zuzu can fix you up with a client. But stay away from The Choreographer, all right?"

"Zuzu?"

The large boy dropped Bolon's arm and tilted his head toward the rotund fourteen year old, who held up a lazy finger. "Zuzu." Then he pointed to himself. "Vay." And then, waving a hand in the air, indicating the smaller boys dawdling behind him: "Strib, Shu, Eggy, Kari, Zef, Zada, Feng, Dajo, Tezca, and Beval. Don't bother remembering their names. They're all interchangeable. Only Cardina knows why there have to be so many."

"Oh." Bolon glanced behind him. And then back at Vay. "I don't need money."

"Good," Vay replied, carrying Bolon's rucksack up a bolted steel incline that led to an enclosed loft-like area, protected from the weather.

When he pushed aside the plastic sheeting insulating the interior of the space, Bolon saw that there were at least thirty small groups of boys—interspersed with a few resilient-looking girls—scattered about the area, talking, encased in sleeping bags, smoking, and sleeping.

Though many of these glanced with respect in Vay's direction as he passed, he paid them no attention. Instead, leading his group, now thirteen boys total, toward a corner of the expanse, he pushed aside another layer of plastic and entered a warm, private room. A stifling room. Unbearably so.

Disregarding the sweat that immediately beaded up on his forehead and cheeks, Bolon examined the place. Wary. Three electric heaters connected to a generator spewed hot air toward the ceiling. The walls were papered with overlapping, illegible posters of lost pets. And the floor was covered with interlocking samples of shag carpeting.

Eight paraffin lamps scattered about the floor provided a milky greenish light. And the carpet discharged a strong, but not unpleasant, aroma of chocolate breakfast cereal. There was also an anomalous wooden wardrobe shoved up against a far wall. Bolon took a small, cautious step forward in aid of a better view.

At the center of the room sat a capacious woman wearing a terrycloth track suit and bedroom slippers. When they entered, she'd been reclined on a futon watching an episode of *The Bob Newhart Show* on an antiquated television set that was also powered by the generator as well as being hooked up to some external cable via a set of cords as thick as Bolon's ankle. Now, she lowered the volume on the television by twisting a knob and looked, mildly interested, in their direction. Vay let the plastic sheeting fall back into place.

After that, still without speaking, he stepped to the center of the room and presented her with Bolon's rucksack. Evoking oddly and insistently to Bolon an illustration from a picture book that he remembered from the time before the breeze had killed his parents–a knight returning from battle. Kneeling before his leader. The other boys, equally subdued, arranged themselves cross-legged in front of the mute television set. Entranced by Bob Newhart.

Cardina extended a hand to accept the rucksack, also peculiarly regal, but she scarcely glanced at it before scoffing, dissatisfied, at Vay. He lowered his eyes.

"Well, this isn't right at all."

Vay nodded, his gaze still on his feet. Silent. As though awaiting punishment.

But no punishment came. Instead, Cardina blew her nose copiously into a wad of tissue she'd extracted from a pocket of her track suit. Paying little attention to Vay or to the other boys. Then, thoughtfully, she stuffed the used tissue into the side of her bedroom slipper.

"Oh well. I suppose you did your best." She half rose to open a door to the wardrobe.

But before she could dispose of the rucksack, Bolon—who had remained standing near the exit, prepared to run if necessary—stopped her. For as the wardrobe had opened, he'd seen thousands of sacks and bags, all packed one on top of the other, more than he'd have thought possible in a piece of furniture of that size. He'd never retrieve his own bag from the mess once she'd abandoned it in there. And she *had* said that it was the wrong one. Perhaps she'd simply return it to him.

Thus, as she made to toss his rucksack onto the pile, he spoke. "Wait. That's mine."

Bemused, she turned her gaze on him. "What's yours."

"The rucksack," he said. "It's mine. They took it from me."

"Mine now." She shrugged, pushed it into the midst of the chaos, and began to close the door. But then, as though feeling something sinister brush her skin, she twisted back toward him. Watchful. "Who are you, anyway?"

Bolon, who was now not only hungry, but also tired and demoralized—thinking above all of his aunt's displeasure at this turn of events—found himself unable to keep his despair in check. He was only twelve. And so, before he could open his mouth to speak, before he could even begin to make his case, two of the paraffin lamps were rapidly blown to the side, igniting the shag carpeting. He covered his mouth with his hand. More than demoralized. Distraught. Paralyzed. And, most of all, ashamed. He felt tears coming to his eyes.

As it turned out, however, little damage ensued. Rather than spreading, the tiny flames were immediately smothered by three of the smaller boys—Zef, Feng, and Eggy, he thought—who whooped with laughter and pounced on the blaze the moment they saw it. Then, still giggling, they rolled back into place in front of the television set. Ignoring the scent of what was now, unmistakably, burnt chocolate breakfast cereal.

To Bolon's astonishment, Cardina was also entertained rather than angered by the accident. Pushing the door to the wardrobe shut, she smiled broadly at him. Wide and warm. Missing a front tooth. "I see. So that's who you are. And you've got some fight in you. Huh." After which, addressing Vay: "he'll do."

Vay raised his eyes to hers. "His name is Bolon."

"Whatever. Works for me." She settled herself back into her futon, lifted her slipper-shod feet to the cushion, and spoke to the crowd of smaller boys. "What did you all do today?" Like a bored schoolteacher.

The tiniest of the group—Shu—raised his hand and simultaneously began speaking. "A man," he said breathlessly, "was painting his house, and I tipped all of his paint cans into the gutter. They made a rainbow. It was pretty." His eyes were bright. Eager to please.

"Good work, Shu." She patted his head. "Stupid man painting a house in November. He ought to know better." Then folding her hands over her belly she nodded to another boy. "And you, Zada?"

Zada toyed with a zipper on his filthy jacket. "Recycling."

"What about recycling, dear?"

"Twenty-three recycling bins. Waiting for the truck." He gave her a shy smile. "All in the river, now. Floating away."

"Away they go," she supplied.

"Away they go," he echoed, with a small laugh. Happy to have earned her praise.

"And well they should," she continued. "If they want the bins to stay put, they ought to secure them properly. Morons."

From there, the discussion became spirited, as the boys spoke over one another, Cardina leading each and every one to describe the petty acts of vandalism in which he'd participated that day. Breaking windows. Ripping roof tiles off houses. Hurling rocks and stones into crowds. Tripping the elderly.

Moreover, after each story, she responded with enthusiasm. Praising some. Encouraging others. Dispensing advice to the few who hadn't met her standards. Until eventually, when all twelve boys had spoken, she clapped her hands and pulled a substantial trunk from under her futon. Bolon couldn't understand how the huge object had fit beneath the chair, but he was beyond questioning at this point.

Rather, he watched as Cardina gestured toward Vay to open it while shouting to the room at large: "Cheez-its and juice boxes for all. More than enough to go around."

After that, she turned up the volume on the television set and ignored them all once more.

Unenthusiastic, Bolon approached the trunk along with the remainder of the boys. He was famished, but he'd also been hoping for something more than convenience store snack food. Unlike the others, therefore, he didn't push his way forward, trying to get his hands on the contents. On the contrary, when they'd all taken their share, he gazed down into the container, uncertain he wanted anything at all.

But Cardina had spoken the truth. Though many of the boys had taken ten or eleven packets of the Cheez-its for themselves, the trunk remained full. Enough for everyone. Endless Cheez-its.

With something that wasn't quite a sigh, he pulled out a packet of Cheez-its and a box of apple juice. Then, hunkering down in a corner of the room—he was uninterested in Bob Newhart—he tore open the snack. Looked with distaste at the orange dust that coated his fingers when he withdrew the first Cheez-it. Wrinkled his nose and inserted the yellow square into his mouth.

But the Cheez-it, he discovered after it had spent less than a second on his tongue, was the most glorious food he'd ever ingested. Filling without being heavy, it flooded his mouth with delicate flavors of sweet and savory unlike any he could remember having experienced. Ambrosia, he vaguely remembered his mother calling food like this. Unmatched. Closing his eyes, he swallowed the tiny square, relishing the feel of it travelling down his throat. And then, greedily, he finished the packet.

Cardina, who had been half watching him, chuckled in his direction when he'd finished.

"Cheez-its," she remarked. "Food of the Gods." She nodded at his unopened box of juice. "Don't forget to hydrate, love. Keeps you strong."

He nodded, eager now, ripped the tiny plastic straw from the side of the box, frowned in irritation when he failed the first few times to puncture the foil circle, and then sucked up the juice in three swallows. The box folding in on itself from the violence of his breath. After which, sated, happy, and secure for the first time since his parents had died, Bolon curled into a ball on a patch of the shag carpet and fell asleep to the sound of Bob Newhart stuttering and the other boys eating. He was looking forward to the morning. He couldn't remember the last time he'd looked forward to the morning.

THE next day, as Bolon trailed Vay—who had been ordered to look out for him—he risked questioning the older boy once again. Though Vay was vexed to have been saddled with a neophyte, he also took a gruff sort of pleasure in demonstrating to Bolon his talent for destruction. Idly ripping the antennas from older cars as they moved past, or raging through a pavement café in the Malaysian district, pulling down the optimistic sun umbrellas lining the exterior (it was November, after all) and overturning a cauldron of soup before bellowing, hooting, and sprinting down the street.

Sometime in the late afternoon, having just toppled a collection of buckets at the edge of a gloomy car wash, Bolon summoned up the nerve to ask him the question that had been bothering him since the viaduct. "What does she do with the bags?"

"I told you," Vay said, still edgy and manic after the episode with the buckets. "She needs them."

"Yes. But what for?" He ran to keep up with Vay, who was now hanging by his hands from a concrete beam supporting an expressway off-ramp. "She threw mine away. I mean, into that wardrobe. She obviously doesn't need all of them."

"Yours wasn't right."

"How do you know which ones are right?"

Vay let himself fall to the ground. "I don't know which ones are right, do I? If I did," he explained with patient contempt, "I'd bring her the proper one, wouldn't I?"

"But–"

"Look," he interrupted. "Her own bag got itself ripped into pieces. Four, five months ago. Some lying, half-cocked Navy Veteran. Addled from the War. And so, now she needs a new one."

"What did she use the old one for?"

"Stop asking idiot questions."

A few minutes later, Vay and Bolon were at the sailing school, surreptitiously capsizing student dinghies. Bolon didn't tell Vay about his history with the place. And in any case, it felt different now. From the other side. He gleefully severed a leech line and watched the snaking sail smack a crying little girl in the face. Giggling.

But when they returned to the squat, and Vay presented Cardina with the bag they'd collected, he began to feel alienated once again. Disappointed by their reception in the overheated room. Disgruntled on Vay's behalf, though Vay himself remained, as before, quiet and stoic.

"No, no, *no*!" She wadded the cotton sack into a ball and shoved it into the wardrobe. "This is the worst one yet."

It was only the Cheez-its that prevented him from fleeing the contagious contempt that very night. Well, the Cheez-its and the chilling thought of his aunt. But the Cheez-its did make everything better. And so, sated and safe once more, Bolon vowed as he closed his eyes to help Vay in his quest. He had a few ideas. The key, he believed, was to go about things systematically.

The next morning, Bolon suggested to Vay that they recruit Zuzu to help them scour spots in the city that might yield up a bag similar to that which Cardina had lost. Rather than grabbing sacks at random from inattentive targets. Vay, reluctantly agreeing that his own strategy hadn't been yielding results, collared Zuzu on the way out. Open, for the moment, to Bolon's less exuberant, methodical approach.

But when Bolon asked them to describe the bag they were replacing, Vay and Zuzu drew a blank. All they could say was that it'd had a feel about it, and that they'd recognize the feel when they handled the material of the new bag. They'd know it when they touched it.

Worse, when Bolon suggested that they collect more than one bag each day to present to Cardina—thereby upping their chances of success—Vay fixed him with a cold, dangerous stare as Zuzu fingered the rusted scalpel he kept in the zippered pocket of his turquoise hoodie. The rule, they said in hollow unison, was one bag per day. One bag only. No more, no less. Bolon, shivering, hadn't pressed them as to why.

But as they approached the first of the neighborhoods they'd scouted earlier—the academic suburb at the edge of the financial district—Bolon lost his fear and began to feel optimistic once again. There was an expectancy in the air that was new to him—something electric—

and when he spotted under an empty bike rack in the University's main square a rotting, mildewed shoulder bag sporting a just-legible public radio logo, he froze. Intrigued.

And then, excited.

Careful, as though approaching a timid wild animal, he crept along the pavement and poked at it three or four times with a stick before, satisfied, he retrieved it. His fingertips tingling. His skin creeping.

Vay and Zuzu, following on his heels, crouched down to see what he'd found. And a few seconds later, they were grinning at one another too. While Zuzu, timid and unlike himself, brushed his fingers against the disintegrating canvas. Stroking it.

But Vay wouldn't allow more than a moment of complacency among his followers. Brusque and frowning, he grabbed the shoulder bag from Bolon, crumpled it into a ball, and crammed it into his pocket. Refusing to admit that it had affected him as it had the smaller boys.

"Fine," he said. "We'll try this one."

When they returned that evening, Cardina was waiting for them, the television already muted, and a strange smile on her face. She, too, Bolon thought, had felt something in the air. Upon accepting the sack, however, she pursed her lips, rueful and amused.

"This isn't it."

Vay's shoulders slumped.

"But," she continued, "it's close. There's a smell about it. You've done well this time, boy."

And then, rather than tossing the rotting sack into the wardrobe with the others, she folded it with care and slipped it beneath her futon. "You've done very well."

The next morning, Bolon, Vay, and Zuzu decided to try the industrial district–that is, the other industrial district, the fashionable one–populated by artists rather than by people like themselves. A wise decision. For once there, it took them little more than a half hour to locate and pounce upon a new candidate for Cardina's replacement sack.

An empty giftbag from the empty Museum down by the river, it was disintegrating into pulp in a small puddle near a drain to the side of a loft conversion. Though disfigured by splotches of paint, and smelling strongly of fish, Bolon could just make out the stylized cuckoo clock mansion in the corner.

Gingerly, he lifted it out of the puddle. Then, shocked, he let it fall to the ground. Wiping his fingers on the front of his shirt.

"There's something inside of it," he said. "Something living. It–it touched me." He felt ill.

Zuzu threw him a condescending look and retrieved the bag himself. Lifted it out of the puddle by the two handles and peeked inside. Curious.

"Water." He wrinkled his nose. "It stinks. Oh. And yeah. There's a worm. With a red dot on its head. Weird looking worm, but kind of –"

"Come on, Zuzu," Vay interrupted. "Dump it, and let's go."

Zuzu looked up from the bag. "Do you think she'll want the worm?"

"No," Vay said, "she will not want the worm."

"But look at it–" Zuzu began, holding out the bag to Vay.

Vay, however, had no patience for wildlife. Grabbing the sack from Zuzu, he dumped the water into the drain without looking at it. And then, all three watched as the worm wriggled at the edge of the grate for thirty or forty seconds until Vay–still impatient–nudged it over the side with the steel toe of his boot.

Tiny as the worm was, Bolon thought he heard it hit the water in the sewer below. A bigger splash than it ought to have made. Along with some ghostly singing? The sound of a flute? But Vay and Zuzu were already striding in the direction of the viaduct, and so, ignoring the sounds coming up from the drain, he ran after them.

Cardina shook her head, impressed, as she examined the damp and filthy gift bag. "Better and better." She glanced up at Vay. "Creative too."

Then she flattened the bag, folded it, and settled it under her futon on top of their offering from the day before. "But still not quite. Good try."

The third morning, Bolon felt feverish. A virus of some sort. And he wasn't certain he could trail Vay and Zuzu all over the city. Especially at their ordinary frenetic pace.

Vay, unusually sympathetic, devised a solution. Rubbing Bolon's filthy hair with his hand, he said, "you know where we haven't looked?"

Bolon and Zuzu shook their heads.

"The construction site under the viaduct. I mean, we picked up Bolon there. But we haven't looked in any of the machines. Or the trailers."

Zuzu rubbed his eyes. Nodded. "Okay."

And so, after prying their way through the hole in the chain-link fence, Bolon, Vay, and Zuzu spent the morning ripping down "danger," "caution," and "no trespassing" signs. Working together, grunting, to overturn a small excavator. Until, bored and fretful, they came upon an empty trailer.

Zuzu suggested they tip that on its side as well, but Vay was looking curiously at the flimsy door. Intrigued, he broke the lock and then, for good measure, tore the door in its entirety from its hinges. "Let's look inside."

Zuzu and Bolon followed Vay up the short, metal staircase. The interior of the trailer was sufficiently wrecked that the three of them couldn't do much more damage than had already been inflicted on the place. Irritated, Zuzu punched a fist through a small, plexiglass window. And Vay, brimming with energy, began fiddling with the knobs on a propane stovetop.

Bolon, however, their quest still in the back of his mind, pushed aside a heap of empty chocolate bar wrappings and pulled an object from beneath a greasy linoleum table. Standing, he displayed it to Vay and Zuzu. A leatherette briefcase branded with the city's logo. Full of something heavy. He could scarcely lift it. The briefcase also stank, palpably, of fear. Bolon could feel the terror seeping into the palms of his hands.

Zuzu lit up, remembering the worm. "What's inside?"

"I don't know–" Bolon began, but Vay snatched the briefcase from him before he could make a guess.

"Who *cares*?" And then, wiping one palm against his trousers while keeping hold of the briefcase with his other hand: "what is that?"

"Fear, I think," Bolon murmured.

"Will she like it?"

"We'll find out." Vay shifted the briefcase to a position under his arm, so that it no longer touched his skin.

"What's inside," Zuzu repeated. Insistent.

"Oh, fuck off." Vay ripped open the briefcase and scattered its contents–thousands of unlimited car wash passes–to the ground.

Zuzu bent over and lifted a card. Peered at it. "Would she want a free car wash, do you think?"

"I said," said Vay, "fuck off."

And, flicking on the propane burner, he fled the trailer, followed by Bolon and Zuzu. They felt rather than heard the explosion as they squeezed their way through the hole in the fence. And Bolon ripped his trousers in his hurry to get away from it. He was certain, despite all evidence to the contrary, that the destruction of the trailer had brought down the viaduct as well. Choking dust was swirling in the air. And the shadow of the expressway was entirely gone.

Cardina, however, was delighted by their day's work. And when they presented the empty leatherette briefcase to her, she rubbed it against her cheek and hugged it to her chest, inhaling. Purring.

"Boys," she effused, "this is—well, still not right. But I love it all the same. Smell it. Have you ever smelled anything like it?"

She shoved the briefcase into Vay's face. Obedient, he inhaled, but otherwise, he showed no emotion.

"I can tell you're close," she relented after a few seconds, clutching the briefcase to her middle once more. "I'm giddy. And," she continued, turning back to the television set, "I plan to sleep with this one tonight."

"I want to ride the tram today." Zuzu's voice was peevish. "I've been helping you. It's my turn to choose where we go."

Vay shrugged and looked at Bolon, who nodded his agreement. And so, that morning, all three entertained themselves by hooting at, shouting into, running after and, occasionally, grabbing hold of the exterior of the charming historic tram that trundled up and down the city's most famous residential boulevard. Looking for all the world like a lithograph of the 1890s—though an 1890s grittier than that which the tram was meant to evoke to the horrified tourists inside, watching the boys and thinking of personal injury litigation.

When the conductor finally managed to chase Bolon, Vay, and Zuzu off, they entertained themselves by appropriating a small, nicely-dressed girl's poodle and tossing it back and forth across the green space beside the tram rail. But when the girl began to cry, Zuzu—to Vay's disgust—felt sorry for her and returned the dog, which seemed excited, rather than put out, by its adventure. Vay nabbed one of the mittens hanging from her coat as they left, insisting to Zuzu that she couldn't possibly need it in mid-November. No snow yet. And in any case, neither she nor the nanny had noticed.

They were enjoying themselves so much that as the sun began to set, they realized that they hadn't located a sack for Cardina. Panicky, all three scoured the tramline, certain that they'd at least find a plastic bag or container from the local convenience store. But, pristine edifice that it was, the tramline didn't suffer litter. Litter was for other neighborhoods.

Zuzu, however, their unlikely savior, who was sniffling to himself in despair, eventually tripped over a small mound beneath the track. Obscured in the failing light. Retrieving it, he ran toward Vay and Bolon, whooping once again with excitement. Euphoric.

"This!" he shouted. "This, this! Look!"

All three stood under a charmingly antiquated streetlamp and examined Zuzu's find. An expensive wallet, bulging with cash, and charred in places, as though someone had dangled it over an open flame. Soot stained Zuzu's fingers where he'd been holding it.

"It's a wallet," Vay observed. "Not a sack."

"Have we got a choice?" Zuzu shoved it at him. "I want to go back. And besides," he added, shrewdly, "it's got the feel about it. Touch it."

Vay didn't respond. Instead, he took the wallet, opened it, removed the cash, and carefully stuffed the banknotes into his pocket.

"It does," Zuzu insisted. "It really does." This to Bolon.

"I believe you," Bolon reassured him. "But I've never felt it. Before, I mean. I wasn't there."

"Yeah," Vay finally conceded, "it does."

Cardina actually giggled when they gave it to her. "That's not a sack."

Vay swallowed and looked at his feet.

"It's *better* than a sack. You're on a roll, kid. Incidentally," she continued as she shoved the empty, scorched wallet into a pocket of her track suit, "was there money in it?"

"No," Vay mumbled to his feet. "None. Just the wallet."

She grinned at him. "Thought not."

The next day, Bolon found their bag before they'd been out for more than an hour. He was getting a sense now of what sort of air to follow. The feeling in his fingertips. They'd returned to the academic suburb, thinking to find something similar to the shoulder bag that was, Vay and Zuzu half-remembered, closest to what Cardina had used before.

Rather than another tote, however, Bolon had come upon a crumpled paper bag from the University bookstore, disintegrating like the Museum's gift bag had been, in a drain to the side of a building. This building, though, was fussy and fastidious rather than brash, constructed of eighteenth-century stone and brick. Moreover, when he looked up from the spot where he'd noticed the bag, he saw that a window on the third floor had been shattered from the inside. As though it, and it alone, had lived through some vicious battle. The rest of the building was smug and untouched.

Vay snatched the bag away from him before he had the chance to examine it.

"Weird." He peeked inside. "It's full of chocolate."

At the mention of chocolate, Zuzu trotted over. "I want some."

"Three bars," Vay said.

Leaning against the side of the building, they sampled the chocolate. And then, simultaneously, they spat it to the ground.

"What the fuck?" Vay was grimacing.

"It must have gone bad." Zuzu, disappointed, dropped the remainder of his down the drain.

"Matcha," Bolon read from the package. "It's infused with Matcha." He paused. "What's Matcha?"

"Who cares? Why would someone do that?"

"Who knows?" Vay muttered, pocketing the sack and turning away. "Same reason they'd smash a window with a dead goat."

"What?" Bolon was running after him.

"You didn't see it? Through the broken window?" He'd shoved his hands into his trouser pockets, and he was pacing quickly away from the square. "A dead goat. A dog too, I think. Rotten and hanging from a tree. They'd been there a long time. Creepy."

"I've got a feeling," Cardina announced, as she examined the bag from the University bookstore, "that tomorrow's the day. You're so close. And I'm so very proud of you."

She actually reached out and patted Vay on the cheek. He remained still and silent.

But as it turned out, Cardina was incorrect. Because in fact it took them three days. And it was only after two mishaps—one with a sodden plastic baggie full of cat and dog figurines that they picked up on the witch hill, and the other with an empty paper sack containing the remnants of pigeon feed that Vay snatched directly from the hand of some delicate grey girl sitting on a bench in the financial district—that Bolon, Vay, and Zuzu found their luck.

Having decided to keep close to home, remaining on the desolate side of the greatly diminished viaduct, Bolon, Vay, and Zuzu entertained themselves at the informal-market street fair, stealing handbags and overturning displays of illegal seconds. Until, surprised and taken aback, all three halted. At the completely unexpected sight of the woman. The proper woman. The woman they'd been seeking all along. Fingering a wristwatch from among a heap of pre-owned Rolexes. Absorbed and inattentive. Her capacious leather bag exposed and accessible at her feet.

"That's it," Zuzu said.

"How do you know?" Vay wasn't going to be pushed. He refused to allow for mistakes.

"Look at it," Zuzu urged him. "It's Gucci."

"It's fake Gucci."

"So what? It's still Gucci."

Vay looked sidelong at him. "That makes no sense at all."

Zuzu shrugged, impatient. "That's the one. You *know* that's the one, Vay."

"Maybe."

Zuzu rubbed his nose. “The lady’s kind of pretty, too.”

Bolon and Vay both stared at him. The woman was squat, elderly, and appeared to be lame. Or, at least, one foot was flat and disfigured. Distending the sneaker she wore.

“What?”

Zuzu continued to gaze at the woman. “Her hair, you know. And, uh, her other stuff.”

Bolon blinked. He thought, for a split second, that he may have seen it. What Zuzu saw. But then it was gone. The woman’s hair was grey and sparse. Her head bald in places. He blinked again. This wasn’t a useful train of thought.

“How will we get it?” He knew that Zuzu was correct. And that Vay was stalling. Losing his nerve.

Vay looked down at him. “You’re small. She won’t see you.”

“Now *you’re* not making sense.”

Vay fixed him with a cold stare. Making clear what he thought of Bolon’s newfound confidence.

“Fine,” Bolon muttered. Knowing his place. “I’ll try.”

Rather than approaching the woman directly, Bolon crept behind the rows of collapsible tables, his eyes on the feet of the vendors, his breathing shallow. And then, when he was behind the man selling the watches, he ducked beneath the table and slowly, carefully, moved in the direction of the woman's bag. Extended his hand toward its large straps.

The moment his fingers made contact, however—sending a jolt of electricity up into his arm—the woman squatted with surprising agility and peered at him under the table. Smiling. Looking a trifle unhinged. She shoved the bag an inch or two in his direction.

"I wasn't doing anything," he blurted out. "I—I was just curious."

"Take it," she said. "You need it more than I do. And I'm in the market for a new bag, anyway. Something to treat myself in my old age." She pushed the bag even closer to him. "I spotted some Fendis across the way there. Nice brand, Fendi."

She paused, thoughtful for a few seconds. "Careful of curiosity, kid."

Bolon remained frozen in place. Certain that her attitude was a trick.

"Take it," she repeated. "I didn't see a thing." Creaking, she stood upright and began haggling with the vendor over the price of the wristwatch she was holding.

And Bolon, unwilling to lose his opportunity, snatched the bag, scuttled backward from the table, and sprinted in the direction of Vay and Zuzu. After that, all three ran like the wind to the squat. Not believing their luck. Not looking back.

THAT night, Bolon slept more deeply than he'd ever slept before—as though he, and not Vay, had been the knight in the half-remembered tale, returned from some impossible quest and deserving of rest. Or relief. Or glory. But when he woke, his desires were mundane. All he wanted that day was to roam the city with Vay and Zuzu, now that all three were free of their obligations. Their city.

Having looked about him upon opening his eyes, however, Bolon saw that he was alone in the sweltering room—alone, that is, aside from Cardina, who was watching *The Price is Right* from her futon. She held the Gucci bag in her lap. Drinking the dregs of a fruit punch juice box.

When she saw that Bolon was awake, Cardina bent forward, turned down the volume of the television set, and smiled at him. "You slept late. Feeling better?"

A pit opened in his stomach, and he jumped to his feet. "Where is everyone?"

"Just you and me now, dear." She stood as well, clutching the straps of the bag.

Without speaking, Bolon backed toward the plastic sheeting, pushed it to the side, and ran into the larger, public area of the squat. But it was empty too. No sleeping bags. No minifridges. Nothing. No one. No resilient girls, even.

At which point, maturity and understanding dawned. Or hit. Like lightning. Nearly shattering him. Though, in the end, as was inevitable, he survived it. The strike.

And so, quiet and deferential, Bolon returned to Cardina's private room. Because he knew that he must. Because to return was his duty. Like the duty of the knight in the story.

Standing in the same place, Cardina was wearing a cloak-like coat over her track suit and a hood-like scarf over her hair. The bag was empty and gaping open beside her on a scrap of the shag carpeting. Waiting for him.

"You coming with us?" She nodded at the bag.

Still silent, Bolon approached and examined the bag. Then, curious despite the other woman's warning, he lowered his face to the opening. Sniffed at it. The interior smelled of Cheez-its. Food of the Gods.

Closing his eyes, he placed one foot inside the bag. And then the other. A small breeze ruffled his hair. Cardina, warm, smiled down on him. Rested the flat of her hand on his head to help him settle.

And then finally, once Bolon was comfortable, she closed and secured the top of the bag, hoisted it over her shoulder and left the room. The squat. The viaduct.

Going elsewhere.

The End

Also From Tiny Boar Books

On the Nature of Things
by T. Edward Abbott

Welcome to the troubled town of Y—ce, where mud and spider silk, bryophytes and hedgehogs' quills have taken on lives of their own.

Things haven't been the same in the village of Y—ce since the forest encroached. A beautiful boy and his sister have developed a taste for wood and eaten their mother's house. The local brewer has purchased a tanned leather sculpture of a disagreeable girl affixed by her feet to a loaf of bread. A cat with reconstructed footpads has transformed an unemployed woman's prospects, though perhaps not in the manner she would have chosen. And an aging widower has found himself bound, literally, to the red lady's slipper orchids he planted over his dead wife's grave…

Evoking Robert Aickman and Neil Gaiman at their sinister best, these interlocking stories of obsession and anxiety, of the uncanny and the illusory, transform the daylight realm of the fairy tale into a murky underworld of horror. As eerie as it is immaculately realized, *On the Nature of Things* is a magical portrait of The Wood in its stripped, unadulterated form.

Exile, or, A Tale of Enchantment in Eight Parts
by T. Edward Abbott

The people of the Republic of Z—rthe have become used to earthquakes. Less so to sudden and acute morphological transformation. But the newly re-opened Consulate of X—ppe is about to change all that.

The Consulate of X—ppe in the Republic of Z—rthe has always been a morose and gloomy place. Now, however, it is also an unstable place, as its functionaries and its attachés, its translators and its hangers-on won't stop mutating. Not enough that the daughter of the Consul General has dwindled to a shriveled, anthropomorphic rock, the size, roughly, of a pint glass. Not enough that a truckload of joyriding Marines, having provoked the ire of a glue-addled little girl, has been transformed into a pod of beached and frantic dolphins. Additionally, a beloved disciple of the Economic Affairs Liaison has developed a skin disease that has left him looking distinctly botanical. Not to mention the tragic and fiery end to the boy who attempted to drive his chauffeur-father's Cadillac.

Like Douglas Adams with a mean streak or Robert Graves in a whimsical mood, T. Edward Abbott has reconfigured eight classic myths of exile and transfiguration into a collection of playful stories shot through with disquieting humor and dark anxiety. A feast of magical disorientation, *Exile* cuts to the heart of what, precisely, is horrible about wishing to become a tree.

The Thirteen Trials of Dr. Marion Bailey
by Felicity St. John

Scholar, spy, and Gothic heroine…Marion Bailey reads like Iris Murdoch or Muriel Spark re-inventing Indiana Jones and George Smiley.

Dr. Marion Bailey has had a checkered career, from the moment she washed up in 1927, a failed scholar blindsided by the brutality of the British Mandate in Iraq to her final adventure in 1938, persecuted by a demonic gibbon conjured up out of a medieval Arabic bestiary. But throughout her tribulations, she's dragged along with her the same traits and wounds: a tortured genius for decoding obscure dead languages, a fragile psyche increasingly battered by each of her exploits, and a tormented responsiveness to the medieval detritus churned up in her wake—and then gobbled up by the British Museum.

Now, in 1967, her forty-year-old son has discovered among this detritus—the five-hundred-year-old Ottoman Book of Kings, the eleventh-century Fatimid pearl of enormous size, the thirteenth-century Ilkhanid celestial globe, and the amorous golem cobbled together by an illegitimate French Queen and a Nabatean magician of ill repute—a manuscript that even his mother refused to touch. As he decides whether to take up the silent challenge posed by the sealed book, he slips backward in time, appraising, finally, his mother's troubled history.

A House in Fragments
by E.M. Hakewessell

A fever dream, a comedy, and an unsentimental portrait of madness, magic, and brilliance, A House in Fragments explores a doomed romance between two pathologically detached people.

High on an island hilltop sits a wood and glass fortress. Built for a genius, it once dominated the surrounding population, human and otherwise. Now an object of ridicule, it houses a lonely recluse barricaded in an attic, terrorized by the possibility of contact with the world. He ventures out only at night to collect stray bits of moss and lichen for what he believes is his art.

Or is it a house at all? To the inhabitants of the island's east shore, it's a driftwood hut. A ruin. Sheltering a hermit in which they only half believe. A madman invented by estate agents out to explain why no one climbs to the invisible summit. Uncongenial to development.

Or perhaps it is neither of those. When a series of inexplicable weather events forces the hermit and a troubled resident of the east shore onto a collision course with one another, both begin to wonder.

A haunting portrayal of what may or may not be mental illness, what may or may not be the thin space between incompatible worlds, *A House in Fragments* is also a story of the marvelous that permeates everyday life—and of the crossing points that sane people dismiss as a trick of the mind.

There's also a petulant faun.

www.ingramcontent.com/pod-product-compliance
Lightning Source LLC
Chambersburg PA
CBHW022100170626
46808CB00002B/524

* 9 7 8 1 9 5 5 2 9 0 0 0 5 *